EXPLORER

DOVE SEASON

ROBIN BRANDE

RYER PUBLISHING

EXPLORER

(Dove Season)

By Robin Brande

Published by Ryer Publishing

www.ryerpublishing.com

Copyright 2025 by Robin Brande

www.robinbrande.com

Cover art by Alex Golke/Deposit Photos

Cover design by Ryer Publishing

All rights reserved.

Print ISBN: 978-1-952383-47-2

Ebook ISBN: 978-1-952383-46-5

ALSO BY ROBIN BRANDE

Dove Season Universe

Dove Season

Finder

Seeker

Believer

Maker

Explorer

Winnie Parsons Mysteries

The Genius Track

A Man of Appetites

A Drop of Sweat

The Long Gray Hook

The Slip of a Rib

Parallelogram Quartet

Into the Parallel

Caught in the Parallel

Seize the Parallel

Beyond the Parallel

Young Adult

Evolution, Me & Other Freaks of Nature

Fat Cat

Doggirl

Replay

Bradamante Saga

Book of Earth

Book of Water

Romance

Love Proof

Freefall

Heart of Ice

Fire and Ice

Collections

The Love of a Good Dog

Mountain Tough

The Miraculous Unknown

Self-Help

What If You're Doing It Right?

What If You're Doing It Right? For Teens

CONTENTS

Dove Season Universe   vi

THE WINDS OF A YELLOW PLANET   I
ON THE SHORE OF A LUNAR SEA   33
THE CANYONS OF A RED DESERT PLAIN   67
THE SOUNDS OF A CRYSTAL PLANET   105
THE GLASS MOUNTAINS OF AN ICE
PLANET   137
THE GRASSLANDS OF PLANET ONYX
GREEN   165
More in the Dove Season Universe   197
About the Author   199
MORE FROM ROBIN BRANDE   201

DOVE SEASON UNIVERSE
RECOMMENDED READING ORDER

Dove Season

Finder

Seeker

Believer

Maker

Explorer

EXPLORER

THE WINDS OF A YELLOW PLANET

1

Sharman Hix still wasn't sure about this. The fact that she had kept it secret from everybody else at the Factory had to be a sign. There was no question that technically she had sneaked the old man out.

But Major Fritz Zimholt had come willingly. Enthusiastically. Maybe even, Sharman was sorry to see, with a feeble kind of desperation.

She only hoped this journey wouldn't end in disappointment. Or worse, disaster.

She loved Fritz Zimholt. Loved him like a father. Over the fifteen years she had worked for him, piloting his experimental aircraft and training other pilots to fly, Sharman had come to think of Fritz as more than a boss, more even than a friend and mentor. He had replaced her family. Father, mother, and brother. Grandparents. The truth was, Fritz had been raising Sharman since she was eighteen. Whoever and whatever she was now, at thirty-three, she had Fritz to thank.

Sharman was already a pilot in high school. She had learned to fly through a program at her elementary school, back when she was only eleven. It was like putting on shoes that were perfectly and especially made for her. All of her flight instructors told Sharman she was a natural. But no one needed to tell her that. Sharman could already feel it from her very first flight. Like she had finally woken up in her right life.

She had her plan. College, advanced science degrees, Air Force, NASA. All on a path to become an astronaut.

Then Major Fritz Zimholt called her just a few days after she graduated from high school, and made her a better offer. A way to reach the stars much faster if she came to live at the Factory, Fritz's hidden facility in the mountains of Utah, to be a test pilot for him.

Best decision of Sharman's life. She couldn't even imagine what the past fifteen years would have been like outside in the regular world. She still missed her family at times—something she never admitted to a soul—but other than that, Sharman was exactly where she wanted to be.

But not if she was going to lose Fritz. Not this soon. He was only eighty-three. People were living past a hundred routinely now, weren't they? Why should Fritz be any different? Sharman still had so much to learn from him about so many things. It was all happening too fast. She wasn't ready.

Until just a few months ago, Sharman wouldn't have thought of Fritz as old. Mature, yes. Wise and experienced.

But still hardy, still tall and imposing, still in command of his body and his mind.

Not anymore. His mind still seemed as sharp as ever—during the fewer and fewer hours he could stay awake—but Fritz's body was a mess. He wouldn't say what it was, but anyone with eyes could see. The dramatic weight loss, leaving his skin bagging on his arms and face. The strange chalky look of his skin. His sunken eyes. His halting gait. Loss of what remained of his white hair.

There were other signs, too, and they all added up. Fritz was dying. And maybe there was nothing anyone else could do.

But Sharman could do something. Maybe. How could she be sure? It was only an idea, a theory. Born of a wild and maybe irrational hope. But even though Fritz didn't say it, Sharman could see it in his reaction: What did he have to lose? What other options did he have?

If she could save him…

But if it didn't work, then he might die even sooner. Maybe even in the next hour.

Could Sharman stand to see that happen? To know that she was the one responsible?

But if she could save him…

Fritz dozed uneasily in the pilot's chair beside her. Sharman had watched the seat mold itself carefully around Fritz, the way it did around any pilot who sat there, but she thought maybe the pod took a little more time than usual. Maybe it sensed the pain in Fritz's bones. Sharman sent her pod a warm thought of gratitude. *Good boy.*

Sharman's relationship with her pod—her connection

to it—had evolved over the past several years. She had always known it was alive and sentient, but she no longer thought of it as a temperamental horse she was learning to ride.

Now she knew it was part of her. An extension of her own body and mind. The man who had originally helped design the pods, Reggie Swan, taught Sharman to think of them as another layer of her own skin.

Sharman no longer needed the lighted circlet she used to wear around her head to communicate with her pod. She could do it easily now, just by tuning in to what she thought of as her pod's particular wavelength.

Once she saw that Fritz looked comfortably settled in the single seat, Sharman asked her pod to make more room and to create a seat for her. The pod smoothly expanded from its single-seater, spherical shape, into a double-wide with a second chair for Sharman. It also raised the dome above them to accommodate Fritz's height. Sharman and Fritz used to think the only people who could pilot the craft had to be small. Under about five foot-seven. But now they understood that the pods would adjust themselves to suit their favorite pilots and passengers. That included Fritz.

No matter what size the pod was, single or double or occasionally even larger, the inside of it was always cozy and sparse. There were no controls. No buttons to press. No levers to push or pull. The lower half of the pod looked gray from the outside, and the top half was a clear dome. The material it was made of rendered it invisible as it flew. Only Sharman's fellow pilots, wearing flight suits made of that same material, could recognize other pods in the air.

Sharman was wearing one of the special flight suits now, in her preferred color of matte gray. It was a nice muted color against her dark skin. She had never dressed for attention, not even when she was younger. She just wanted to study and learn and fly. Then and now.

Fritz wore a black flight suit that made him look like a scuba diver. He had the hood pulled up over his bald head and he wore the pliable black boots that were a standard part of the kit. Both of their flight suits fit them like a comfortable second skin and kept their bodies at a perfect temperature. And the material made the two of them as invisible as the ship. It was some kind of alien tech. Fritz had never told her more about it than that.

Sharman pulled up the thin hood of her suit and snugged it around her face. She tucked away the few stray curls of her short black hair. She reached down and removed her pliable black boots and stowed them at the side of the footwell. Then she settled into her seat.

As the chair began its process of molding around her, fitting her perfectly underneath her bent arms and around her torso and legs, Sharman spread her bare toes against the raised platform that angled toward her at the base of her feet. She liked to feel the pod, skin to skin. She always thought it made a better connection.

Sharman spoke inside her mind and gave her pod the coordinates of where she wanted to go. Then she added the step Reggie Swan had taught her when he came to visit several years ago. It was an advanced mental maneuver.

Something Reggie said he learned from three extraterrestrial friends of his. He called it mental physics. A way that Sharman could tune her mind and heart into a kind of universal time map, to direct the craft straight where she wanted it to go without having to traverse any distance in space. They would arrive in an instant, like the snap of a rubber band.

Even though she knew the exact coordinates of the spot where she wanted to take Fritz on the yellow planet, she wanted to let him see the whole planet first, from a distance, to take it all in.

Sharman knew Fritz was like her, always wanting to savor the wonder of a new experience. Fritz had a scientific, mechanical mind, but he was also a lover of beauty and the mysteries of the universe. She wouldn't cheat him of this.

"Fritz," she said gently. "Fritz. We're here."

The old man roused himself. He blinked a few times, trying to focus.

Then he pushed himself upright in his seat. A smile broke across his face. Sharman smiled just to see it.

Overall, the planet in front of them was a strange mustard yellow. It had darker patches in certain areas, dark brown, some of them black where a lava-like layer extended beneath some of the many dead volcanoes Sharman and her five-person crew had found here on their first visit just two days ago.

The planet had enough of an atmosphere that Sharman could see a thin film of cloud or mist in a section over to her right. Although considering the high winds on the planet surface, it could just as easily been pockets of dust storms or even tornadoes stirring up the powdery yellow dirt.

From here it was hard to see how rugged the surface of the planet was. A mixture of hard-packed dirt and rock, with a thick layer of loose, fine dust coating everything. The constant heavy winds kept the dust swirling and churning, reducing visibility to just a few feet in any direction.

Rising from the yellow, dusty plains were thousands of bare, rocky mountains. Interspersed among them were an equal number of dead volcanoes, some of which had once spewed their black lava across the plains and down into the valleys. If it had ever been habitable or hospitable, it certainly wasn't now. It was a dead planet covered with dead volcanoes.

A dead planet except for the one spot where Sharman was taking Fritz now.

Let him see for himself. Let him decide for himself. Sharman couldn't make that decision for him. Her whole plan involved a terrible level of risk. There was no guarantee it would work. No guarantee at all. In fact, there was probably only the slimmest chance that she could pull it off.

But they had come this far. She should at least show Fritz the place. If they turned around after that and went back to the Factory, no harm, no foul.

But if she lost her nerve now, she'd never forgive herself. Fritz should be the one to decide.

He stared out through the dome of the pod, surveying

with apparent delight the mustard-colored planet before him. "What did you call it?" he asked.

The question surprised her. It wasn't Sharman's place to name the planets. That was for people on the science team. And as far as she knew, they were still calling it by a collection of letters and numbers. C5V-46. The plan was to come back here and map it, explore further over a series of more visits. But Sharman didn't want to wait for that. She saw what she saw. And immediately thought of Fritz.

"Why don't you name it?" she said. It seemed right that he should.

"I'll think of something," Fritz said. His eyelids made the kind of slow blink that signaled he might be falling asleep again. Sharman hated to see it. This vigorous man, so changed.

She needed to hurry up while he still had any energy to bring to the effort. Sharman couldn't see from here the place where she wanted to take him. And she didn't want to risk flying the pod through whatever that atmosphere below was made of. But she didn't have to. There was an easier way to do it.

Sharman knew the coordinates. She told her pod. It snapped them to the planet's surface.

The pod landed on a hard, flat plain where the yellow dust swarmed. The ferocious wind blew horizontally in this section and pelted the fine sand against the clear dome at the top of the pod. Sharman could feel the high winds rocking her craft. For the moment she stayed where she was.

Fritz had fallen asleep again, just in the silent space of

the past few minutes. She felt reluctant to wake him. Fritz's forehead was creased in a frown. Was he in pain? Having a nightmare? He moaned. That was enough. Sharman covered the top of his vein-lined hand with her own.

"Fritz?" she said softly. "We're here. Let's suit up and go out."

2

———

Their head gear was a strange piece designed by Reggie Swan. When Sharman first met Reggie, nine years ago, all she saw was a fit old black man, maybe in his seventies or so, with skin as dark as hers and a mass of hair threaded through with lots of gray. She had no idea at the time what a brilliant mind lay beneath those gray hairs.

Reggie brought a friend with him that first day.

Commander Sharman Hix. An older Sharman. Some future Sharman. Twenty-four-year-old Sharman got to meet her future self.

Older Sharman couldn't stay long, she had spaceship commanding to do—a fact that current Sharman still clung to and reminded herself of only about twenty times a day.

But Reggie Swan stayed on. He had a lot to discuss with Fritz. And in the almost year that he stayed, he taught Sharman a lot about the pods he had designed for Fritz back in the day.

Reggie also made some new equipment for the future work he knew Fritz and Sharman and others at the Factory would be doing one day.

And that equipment included the head gear Sharman helped Fritz put on and activate while they were still safely inside the pod.

Like the pods, the head gear was alive. Alive and thinking for itself.

It was made of the same clear material that formed the upper domes of the pods. It was transparent, light weight, unscratchable, unbreakable.

It took Sharman a while to understand that Reggie wasn't *building* with that material, wasn't constructing a piece of gear, he was *growing* it. Like cells in a Petri dish. Like the kind of spare body parts that can now be grown in laboratories just from the smallest sample of human tissue.

Reggie talked to his growing head gear. He talked through what exactly he wanted to accomplish. Something light weight, indestructible, and something that would mold itself to each individual wearer, the same way the pods' seats molded to the shape of their pilots.

It had to preserve life. It should maintain the perfect atmosphere inside the clear dome so that the person wearing it could breathe as easily as standing at sea level on Earth.

It had to keep out whatever noxious gases or choking atmosphere might surround the person on another planet, outside the pod, wherever they happened to be.

It had to provide superb visibility. In darkness, it lit up. In direct light, it darkened to protect the eyes.

In pelting dust storms, like this one, or in snow storms or rain or whatever might obscure the wearer's sight, the head gear shed the particles before they could accumulate.

Visibility might still be limited, like it was on the surface of the yellow planet, but only because the dust filled the air so thickly it was impossible to see more than a few feet ahead. But it wasn't the head gear's fault. Sharman never had to wipe her hand over it or shake the powdery dust off. Almost as soon as the dust touched the head gear, the material cleared it away.

And last, the head gear had to fit as comfortably as the flight suits. It had to fit slimly to the head—not a big bubble, like a helmet—so that the wearer could climb, run, even swim without ever having to worry about the head gear getting in the way or in any way holding them back.

And so what Sharman pressed against Fritz's forehead now was a simple gelatinous sheet of the thin, raw material. Like putting on a sticky note that covered the length of his face.

"Breathe," Sharman reminded him. "One breath in and out."

It was the out breath that mattered. The material took information from both the wearers' skin and from their exhalation. Fritz drew in a shallow breath and overemphasized the exhale. It made him start to cough. But the head gear didn't mind that. It was busy doing its work.

In half a minute it had constructed a protective sheath around Fritz's head. It was shaped to his individual features and sat just beyond the surface of his skin. Whatever filtering system Reggie had created, Sharman still didn't understand. All she knew was that there was plenty of room to breathe easily and she never felt like she was suffocating or overheating.

She applied one of the short ends of a second gelatinous sheet to her own forehead. She kept the hood of her flight suit in place, covering the back of her head and the edges of her face up to where the outside edges of her eyebrows began.

Sharman took a breath in and blew it out. The head gear grew into its finished form. Sharman took another few breaths, just to test it, although she knew by now that she could trust it. For all the head gear she had tested over the past several years, not a single one of them had failed.

Granted, most of the tests had been done while she was still flying in the Wasatch Mountain Range outside Salt Lake City. But she had tested it through wind and rain and snow, tested it at night and in bright sunlight. The head gear did what Reggie said it would do. Sharman had faith in the designer and in what he grew.

Sharman pulled her boots back on. Then she turned to Fritz and placed her hands on his shoulders. She looked him in the eyes.

"It's awful out there," she said. "The wind's going to knock you down. It almost carried me away."

Fritz smiled at that. Sharman was as petite as a pixie. But Fritz didn't say that a puff of air could carry her away.

Instead he nodded. He understood. He was letting her call the shots. It made Sharman feel strange. Strange and sad. Fritz should be in charge. But he couldn't be. Not the way he was now.

Maybe on the return trip. She hoped it with all of her heart.

"You hold my hand, understand? Never let go."

Fritz nodded. He wasn't smiling anymore. He looked tired. Tired and sick and worried. But also ready. Determined. He was with her. He wasn't backing down.

"Okay," Sharman said, "here we go."

The lid of the pod slicked back into the lower edge of the frame. Dust came storming into the craft.

"Make it fast!" Sharman shouted to be heard above the wind. She helped Fritz climb out. He wasn't steady. She had to do a lot of the lifting.

She told the pod to close up, quickly. It slicked its dome lid up and over again. Sharman stood outside the pod gripping Fritz's hand tightly, holding him close against her side.

His grip was weak in return. His legs looked shaky. She had brought the pod as close to the phenomenon as she dared. She didn't want to risk landing on top of it.

One step, two, three, she had already paced it out a few days ago. Just ten steps. The wind beat against her body and her head. It wanted to get into her flight suit, into her eyes and mouth, but everything she wore held tight and kept the dust and pelting sand away.

There was no point in asking Fritz if he was doing all right. She would have had to shout it, and what if the answer was no? She was still going to keep dragging him forward, leaning into the ferocious wind. There was no going back. Not yet. Just a few more steps—

And then they entered the wind break that Sharman

had found two days ago. Like pushing through a curtain hanging over a door to a place where suddenly everything was quiet and still.

Over on this side, the winds had other work to do. They couldn't waste time pummeling two puny humans who dared to intrude upon the planet.

In the sudden stillness, Sharman caught her breath. She could see Fritz's chest heaving. His hands and legs were trembling. Those ten arduous steps from the pod to here had taken all of his strength.

But he didn't seem to notice. Who could, in the face of what he saw?

Sharman watched Fritz as he watched the phenomenon. One cycle, a second, a third. Just to believe that what he saw was true. Sharman had watched it half a dozen times at first for that very same reason.

"Dear God," Fritz murmured.

Sharman answered, "I know."

3

On a dead yellow planet filled with dead volcanoes and dead bare mountains and plains covered in nothing but powdery yellow dust, there was, after all, life.

Right here, right where they stood. A patch of green as large as a soccer field. Green ... sometimes.

A low shrub grew here. It had short, fleshy leaves, and small bulbous sacs that grew from the stalks and looked like they might contain water or some other liquid. Maybe only a few tablespoons per sac. Sharman hadn't dared pluck one or squeeze it to find out. She couldn't imagine interfering with the cycle.

If green plants grew here, it must mean there was water underground. But the green growing plants weren't her only clue.

The cycle progressed like this. The soil beneath the plants looked moist. Like someone had watered it lightly, for just a few minutes. Not long enough for the water to sink down, to penetrate. Just a little sprinkling.

The sprout of the plant emerged from the moist yellow soil. Very quickly. In maybe two or three seconds. It continued to grow upward, then outward, adding leaves, adding sacs. That took about five seconds. Maybe seven.

It reached its full height of about twelve inches. It was bushy by then, with lots of the little sacs. Call it another five to seven seconds.

Then the water at its base began to dry. The soil cracked. The plant died. Three seconds, maybe five. Very fast. Dead, it dried into a russet red. The sacs dried and burst open. Spores flew out. The circular winds carried the spores in a loop, where they fell upon the dry ground, then the ground moistened again, then a sprout came up, and the entire cycle repeated.

At most, from birth to death to rebirth, a cycle took about twenty-five to thirty seconds. Over and over. As the winds blew, carrying the spores or the seed pods or what-ever the plant created. A whirlwind that produced life. Then death. But then life again, over and over.

Was it the wind or the plants? Sharman had watched the phenomenon as long as she could before the rest of her team returned. Somehow she didn't want to show them. Not yet. She didn't include it in her notes.

Because the idea had already come to her, come racing into her mind.

If she could bring Fritz here.

Let him somehow put himself in the way of those cycling winds.

It was crazy. But she couldn't shake the idea. She just knew it could be the answer.

So he was the first person who saw it, other than her. She didn't want to influence him. She needed to know his unfiltered thoughts.

"What do you think this is?" she asked.

Fritz watched another full cycle before he answered.

"I don't know," he said. "I'm not sure." He was still holding her hand. She could feel him shake.

She had to cut straight to it. They couldn't just stand here forever. "Is it the plants themselves or is it the wind?"

Fritz watched in silence two more cycles.

"The wind," he said. "The plants are trapped in it. If not for the wind, they would have died and dried up like everything else on this planet."

"Exactly," Sharman said. It was her analysis, too.

"And the moisture," Fritz said. "It wouldn't be there anymore. It would have dried up long ago. But somehow the wind keeps freshening it. Keeps it returning." He watched another cycle, then turned to Sharman. His eyes looked bright and alive. There was a new vigor in his expression.

"So tell me," he said. "What do you think I can do?"

"I ... Fritz, I'm not sure about any of this."

"Understood."

Now that he was here, now that the moment was at hand, Sharman was afraid to commit. To suggest what she had in mind. She wanted it to come from him. She wanted it to be his idea.

And now she wondered whether she shouldn't have

brought Caroline Baird along after all. She was Fritz's oldest friend at the Factory and she was his senior scientist. But Sharman felt certain that Caroline would have said not to do it. That it wouldn't work, that it wasn't what Sharman thought, it couldn't be the wind—all the objections had swirled in Sharman's head over the past two days, making her want to just sneak Fritz out on his own and see whether he thought it was anything that could help him, or whether the whole idea was too crazy.

"I think I would have to strip down," Fritz said. "Down to skin level."

So he was really thinking of doing it. He saw it the way she did.

"No head gear," she said. "I think you're right. And that's a whole separate risk. You can't breathe this air."

"But the cycle is fast," Fritz countered. "I can hold my breath that long."

"We don't know how the atmosphere might affect your skin," she countered. "What if it's poisonous?"

Their flight suits protected them from any of that. If Fritz was right—and Sharman thought he was, she'd had that same idea about him needing to strip down—then the risk of exposure might outweigh the so far very theoretical benefit of standing in the stream of that wind.

A lot to consider. And none of it guaranteed.

The temperature was bearable. Only about ninety-eight degrees. A mild summer afternoon where Sharman grew up in Phoenix, Arizona. So at least that shouldn't pose a problem.

"I don't know, Fritz. This has to be your decision. I'm not sure about any of it. This is all completely new."

"I don't have a lot of time for research," Fritz said. "As I'm sure you've guessed." He squeezed Sharman's hand. She squeezed his back.

"How do you think I should do it?" he asked. "Leave the head gear for last?"

"It all has to be fast," Sharman said. "Be ready to go right before the start of a new cycle. And the least possible exposure before that. I'll have to help you take it all off. But let's plan it first."

They agreed that for modesty's sake he would leave on his briefs. Maybe that was stupid, Sharman wasn't sure, but she couldn't make herself pretend that seeing her mentor and father figure naked was no big deal. It was.

But really, was it? If it meant the difference between him getting the full effects of the wind, or not?

Damn it, get over it. "Fritz, I think you have to strip down all the way. I won't look. Trust me."

Fritz nodded. Sharman thought maybe he was embarrassed, too. But they weren't children and this was too important to botch just because of her sense of modesty.

They rehearsed the sequence: the boots, the hood, the suit, the underwear, and last, quickly, the head gear.

Step into the stream of the wind at the very beginning of the cycle. Stand right over one of the plants. Arms extended from his sides to get maximum coverage against his skin. Hold his breath. Wait for the apex of when the other plants grew to their full height and width, then step out of the wind before it moved on to the death cycle, to the drying of the ground and the plants and the spreading of the spores.

"You have to get out of it in time," Sharman said. "You can't stay in there a half-second too long. You understand that, right?"

Fritz nodded. He was watching another cycle, no doubt trying to plan the right time to move in and the right time to escape. Like some action film where the hero had to rush between the spinning blades of an industrial fan to outrun the villain and not get sliced up in the process.

"Fritz…" Sharman waited until he gave her his attention. "I'm just not sure about any of this."

He smiled. A gentle, fatherly smile that was meant to reassure her. But there was a shadow behind his gaze that Sharman couldn't ignore.

He was sick. He was weak. He might be despairing of his chances back on Earth. Did that mean she should indulge him by throwing him into the blades of a spinning fan?

But why else had she brought him here? If there was a chance to save him, she had to try. Even if Caroline Baird or any other scientist or level-headed advisor might say this was the worst idea in the world.

Fritz had taken plenty of risks in his life. Sharman took them every day flying the experimental aircraft—and now spacecraft—that Fritz had developed in his mountain hideout. They were both brave and maybe foolish people, but it had gotten them this far. Standing on a dusty, windy yellow planet where there was still an oasis of life on this strange green sward.

"Let's get ready," Fritz said. He reached down and pulled off his boots. Sharman's heart started hammering. Her breath sped up. They were really going to do this. Oh, man.

Boots off, Fritz stood watching the middle of the current cycle. "Let's let a few more go by," he said. "Come on, though, let's hurry." He removed his head gear just long enough to pull down the hood of his flight suit. Head gear back on while he continued stripping the suit off his shoulders and chest.

Sharman helped him keep pulling it off. She peeled it like a used glove. She could turn it right side out again once he was out of it. For now they needed speed.

They stripped him completely naked. Sharman had no trouble averting her eyes. She knew she was being too sensitive. If she was a doctor or nurse, she wouldn't care.

Fritz was scrawnier than she knew. He had lost much more weight than she suspected when she saw him in his clothes. His skin looked papery and loose and an unhealthy shade of grayish-white. He didn't look strong at all anymore. He was a frail old man.

But frail or not, old or not, dying by the day, Fritz still stood upright and alert, feet poised to give him a running start, and he held his hand over his head gear, ready to strip that off last and run into the whirlwind.

"Let me count it," Sharman said. Her palms were sweating inside her suit. She stared at the nearest bush, the one where Fritz would run in and stand over. The bush was at its fullest point now. Any second it would begin to die back.

"Okay, get ready!" Sharman said. She gripped Fritz's arm, ready to launch him. "Mask off!" He stripped it away. "Almost! Okay, NOW!"

She pushed Fritz into the swirling wind. He straddled the bush and spread his arms.

Sharman's eyes jerked from Fritz to the plant beneath him, back to Fritz, back to the plant.

Moist soil. Fritz standing tall. Sprout popping up. Fritz. Now the leaves. The first few sacs. Then more. Fritz with his back to her, so she couldn't see his face, but he wasn't shaking anymore. He stood firm.

She couldn't risk calling out to him, asking if he was all right, asking what was happening. She didn't want to distract him, didn't want him to move. Not yet. It was almost time to jump out.

"Get ready!" she called. "Almost!" She didn't know if he could see the other plants from where he was looking. It might be her call alone. She had to get this right. She couldn't let Fritz stay a quarter-second too long and over-stay the life cycle.

"Almost ... NOW!" Sharman reached out and grabbed Fritz and yanked him out of the wind.

He bent over and braced his hands against his knees. He wheezed. He looked bad. He looked frightened. He looked shaken.

Sharman held the head gear back up to his face. It remolded itself around his head. Even without his hood and his flight suit on, the head gear sealed against his skin and reactivated so Fritz could breathe. He took several heaving breaths. Sharman didn't like the sound of any of them. And being exposed like this wasn't helping. She needed to get him suited up again.

"Fritz, we need to get you dressed." His eyes were wide, maybe panicked. But he nodded. He understood.

Sharman helped him with his briefs. It was hard for him to stand on one leg at a time. He leaned against her for support. Dressing him wasn't going to be easy.

The flight suit was skin tight. It wasn't something she could pull over his legs while he leaned against her. He would likely fall. He needed to put it on himself. But he didn't seem capable at the moment. This wasn't going to work. Sharman didn't know if Fritz was any better, or maybe even worse. She had to do what she could and then get him back to the pod.

"Just put on your boots," she told him. She helped him step into one at a time and pulled them up over his ankles. "Come on. Come with me." She grabbed his hand and carried his clothing under her opposite arm and pulled him back out into the ferocious horizontal wind.

After the quiet of the oasis, the noise was shocking and unnerving. The wind was at their backs going in this direction, but that didn't make it any easier. It pushed them, it pelted them with the fine yellow dust and obscured the view beyond just a foot in front of them. But it was just ten steps to the pod, ten plodding, difficult steps. Sharman called out to the pod with her mind and told it to get ready the moment it sensed her.

The pod waited until the last moment, then slid open for Sharman and Fritz to clamber back inside. The pod closed itself tight again. There was yellow dust all over the seats and the walls and the floor.

Fritz heaved a sigh and collapsed back against his seat. Sharman could see his thin chest rising and falling with each breath. He seemed as frail as ever. But then she raised her gaze to his eyes.

He was staring at her with an electric kind of intensity Sharman had never seen on his face before. As though some fire burned behind his brown irises, making them seem burnt orange around the black pupils.

"Fritz? Are you all right?" Sharman's voice sounded younger than she was anymore. But she knew it was because she was scared. She didn't know whether Fritz was well or closer to death. She gripped his hand. "Tell me!"

Fritz let out a throaty laugh. More like a bark than a man's laugh. He squeezed Sharman's hand. She could feel the strength returned to his fingers. She could feel the life flowing back into his veins.

There was color on his cheeks. Two high bright patches of rose, like he had a slight fever. His eyes looked brown again, not that strange fiery orange. For a moment he had looked possessed.

Fritz reached down and removed his boots again, then began pulling on his flight suit. As he did the words came tumbling out. Not halting, not weak, but strong and sure. "Yes, I'm all right. By God, I'm cured."

Sharman stared at him, wanting to believe it. Such a simple statement. *By God, I'm cured.*

"How do you know?" she asked anxiously. "How can

you say that?" Her heart fluttered with a mixture of hope and fear. She didn't want Fritz to be wrong.

"It's not the wind," Fritz said. "We were wrong about that. Or at least it's not only the wind. That was time, Sharman. It's a loop of trapped time."

Sharman gave her head a sharp shake. Not from disbelief, but because she didn't understand.

Fritz finished pulling the flight suit up over his shoulders. He tugged the hood back over his bald head.

"What if we were caught in a loop right now?" Fritz said. "What if as soon as I finished dressing, I was naked again? And over and over I put on my flight suit, then it disappeared, then I put it on again. It would be because I'm caught in a time loop. The winds outside wouldn't have anything to do with it. In fact, now that I say it, it's clear that they're caught in that loop, too."

Now the light was dawning. Sharman took it from there.

"So the wind blows." She passed her hand from left to right in front of her in the pod. "Horizontally, just like the other wind we had fight through. But over there, in the oasis, let's call it, it returns to the left and blows right again. Over and over."

"Not a circle," Fritz confirmed. "We just assumed that because it makes sense from what we've seen before. We've never seen winds on Earth that blow in a repeating horizontal path."

"And so the plants," Sharman said. "They're caught in the loop, too. And the soil. All of it. A moment in time, but what … sped up?"

"Plants don't grow and die in half a minute," Fritz said. He shrugged. "Or maybe they do here. But whatever the time line was before, they all got trapped. They live and die over and over."

"And ... so what does that mean for you?"

Fritz was silent for a moment. Sharman turned to stare out at the swirling yellow dust. This planet was inhospitable. It could not sustain life. At least not human life.

And yet it deserved investigation. Sharman still wanted to return here with her original crew. And maybe ask Caroline Baird to come, too. Let her see the oasis for herself.

But not until Fritz explained what happened to him. Sharman still didn't understand exactly what occurred. How could Fritz declare himself cured? It seemed too easy. Even though it was exactly what Sharman hoped would happen. She should be elated. And yet she still wasn't sure.

"Tell me what you noticed about the plants," Fritz said. "About the stages they went through in the cycle."

"I'm sure it's the same that you saw," she said. "They sprouted, they grew, they dried up and died, their dry spores went into the air and the sprouts grew from them again."

"Exactly," Fritz said. Then he waited. As if Sharman had just given herself the answer. But she still didn't understand it. She didn't have a clue.

"When did I join the cycle?" Fritz asked.

"Right at the beginning. Right when the soil looked moist. Before the sprouts came up."

"We timed it right," Fritz said. "*You* timed it right. You

sent me in there just in the nick of time. What was my body when I entered the time loop?"

"Sick," Sharman said. "Dying."

"That was point zero," Fritz said. "So follow the line."

He drew a horizontal line through the air between them. Sharman stared at it, trying to solve the puzzle.

"Point zero," she said. "Sick. Point one, new life, sprouting from the soil."

"Where did that life start?" Fritz said. "It wasn't just the soil."

"No," Sharman said, "it was the spores."

"The dried, dead spores," Fritz said. "Carried on the wind back into the dry soil that was about to become wet."

Sharman closed her eyes and tried to see it. Tried to see the time loop of the plants and the soil and what it meant for Fritz.

"It's the death," she said. "Isn't it? That's where you came in, too."

"The dried, dead spore," Fritz said. "There just in time to catch life before it began again for every life form caught in the loop."

Sharman could see it in her mind. Fritz's body as the drifting spore. Showing up at the exact right moment, seeding the new plant just when the soil was ready to nourish it. If not for the death there would be no life.

Timing was everything. She had gotten lucky. A split second earlier or later, she would have missed it.

"So it cured you?" she asked. "How? It ... grew a new you?"

"There was no death. You got me out in time. There

was only life. The disease isn't here right now. It comes later." Fritz drew his finger across the air again. "Over here. But I never got there. You pulled me out in time."

Sharman took it in. It didn't make sense in her earthly world. But they weren't on Earth right now. And Reggie Swan had a theory that the physics on their home world might not be the same everywhere else. Maybe that was true of time. And of life and death, too.

There was no question that the man sitting beside her in the pod wasn't the same frail, sleepy old man she had brought out here. Fritz seemed vibrant again. Awake and alive. It wasn't her imagination. The change was real. Fritz felt it, too. Sharman was beginning to believe him.

Somehow she had found the exact right time in the sequence. He didn't have to die to be reborn. Being close to death was near enough.

There was a lot Sharman still didn't understand about what had happened. But she had time now to figure it out. She wasn't racing to save Fritz's life.

"What are you going to call this place?" Sharman asked him. She sent a thought to her pod to take them home.

"You name it," Fritz told her. "You found it."

The pod snapped them back to the mountains of Utah, where the sky was blue, not swirling with yellow dust. Where the towering conifers and the wildflowers suddenly looked more vibrant and colorful than ever. Sharman feasted her eyes.

It was how she wanted to think of the yellow planet. Not the swirling dust, not the dead volcanoes, not the dry and dead yellow plains.

She wanted to celebrate the green patch of life she had found trapped in a pocket of wind. The patch of time trapped on the distant planet, endlessly restoring life from death.

"Let's call it Oasis," Sharman said.

Fritz smiled. She could tell he approved.

He had created a time loop of his own, whether he saw it that way or not. Fifteen years ago Fritz Zimholt had plucked a young pilot off the path she had planned to take, and instead brought her to this distant place to show her a bigger world.

A bigger universe. One she was learning to travel through now, using inventions her younger self never could have envisioned.

And today she had used her skills to bring Fritz to another planet where he could be healed. A completed loop.

Sharman would go back to Oasis. Soon. Maybe sometime in the next few days. Bring her team with her again. Learn more about the yellow world. Map it for future travelers who wanted to explore it for themselves.

But for now she just wanted to take Fritz home. He wasn't frail and exhausted anymore, but after all they had been through, both of them needed a rest.

But Sharman could already feel the urge to leave her home planet again. Maybe tomorrow. Travel outward and find out what else was there.

ON THE SHORE OF A
LUNAR SEA

ON THE SHORE OF A
LUNAR SEA

Julie Trident had her orders. But sometimes the chance of discovering something new meant you couldn't wait for updated instructions.

Sharman Hix, the team leader for this expedition, had been clear: Survey the moon of the yellow planet they were calling Oasis. Do not set foot on it. Do not explore on your own. This was a mapping expedition, nothing more. Do not be tempted, no matter what.

But Julie was tempted. Beyond tempted. And she wasn't in the military anymore. She wasn't working for a governmental agency. In fact, she wasn't working for anyone. Her position with Sharman Hix's team was, technically, voluntary. Which meant Julie was a free agent. Sharman couldn't give her orders, so much as just make suggestions.

At least that was what Julie was trying to convince herself of as she gazed out the top dome of her pod and stared in wonder at the sight below.

Dr. Julie Trident was there as a science advisor. And maybe as muscle in case it was needed. No one had said that explicitly, but Julie was a former Marine as well as a scientist. People must see her as a double asset. Even if she wanted more than anything else to leave her fighting life behind.

It was her science life that she wanted to resurrect. It was why she had come back to the Factory, the hidden facility in the Wasatch Mountain Range near Salt Lake City, Utah, where her mother was the senior scientist.

And then Julie found out what kind of work her mother was doing these days.

Impossible to resist.

Julie had never conceived of going into space. It wasn't even on her radar. It had never been one of her dreams.

But people from the Factory, the pilots of these experimental craft like the pod Julie was sitting in right now, had solved the problem of space-time travel and were ready to go out into the wild black yonder of uncharted space and begin charting it. Like the first sailors risking everything to take ships out onto the sea.

"They need scientists," her mother had told her. "I would go if I could. Believe me."

Julie did believe her. And she pitied her mother for not being able to do it. But Dr. Caroline Baird had been functionally blind for several years now. And she was old. Julie hated to admit it, but the evidence of her eyes didn't lie. Her mother was only sixty-four now, but it wasn't a hardy sixty-four. She looked and acted twenty years older than that.

But Julie was young and strong. Only thirty-seven. Plenty of years to explore. And maybe only a few of those years for her to have the chance to tell her mother about everything she saw. Wasn't it the right thing to do? Even if Julie didn't already have her own burning curiosity about what Sharman Hix's expedition team might find, it just seemed too precious of a chance to pass up, when it would make Julie's mother so happy.

So Julie took the necessary steps. She had never flown any kind of craft before—she had never wanted to—but she asked Sharman to teach her.

It wasn't like a plane or any other kind of aircraft, Sharman said. These pods are living, thinking creatures. We don't own them. We don't boss them. We're their partners, if we're lucky enough that they'll have us.

For the past year Sharman had been teaching Julie how to pilot the strange living craft. Each pod was large enough for just one pilot. At five-foot-seven, Julie Trident was at the upper range of what the Factory normally considered the ideal height for a pilot. Sharman Hix was several inches shorter. When Sharman rode in her pod Julie could see plenty of head room above her up to the curve of the clear dome.

When Julie piloted her own, she had, at most, about two inches of space above her. But despite that, the pod seemed to mold itself around her and feel comfortable, not claustrophobic. Like a cozy bubble all around her, no bigger or smaller than it should be.

The pods were sphere-shaped. Their lower halves looked dark gray on the outside. The upper halves were clear, allowing a three hundred sixty-degree view. Inside the pod the lower half was a golden-rose, softly metallic color. It was solid to the touch, and yet at times felt almost pliable beneath Julie's soft black boots as they pressed against the raised and angled foot platform and as she pressed her fingers into the ends of her armrests.

The pods had no visible controls. No way to steer or accelerate or brake. That was what took Julie the longest to learn: how to rely solely on mental communication with her pod, asking it to travel this way or that, go up, go down, slow, go faster, please stop.

None of it felt natural. Even Sharman admitted that there were still things she was learning about how best to pilot the pods. And she had been doing it for fifteen years.

Small consolation on the days when Julie spent most of her time flying upside down, and not on purpose.

But she was better at it now, after a year of constant training. Reliable enough that Sharman had trusted Julie to circumnavigate this moon on her own. The rest of the team, Sharman plus four others, were down on the planet Oasis mapping out their own designated sections. There was much more surface area down there. This moon was a little thing in comparison.

Only about thirty miles in diameter, the moon hadn't even shown up on any of the earth-bound scans. They didn't know it was here until they came out to the yellow planet in person. Then surprise, here it was.

This was only the team's second time visiting the planet. Sharman's instructions took that into account.

"This is a marathon," she told the five of them. "We

might come out here fifty times this year. You don't have to get it all at once. Slow is pro. Don't rush it."

All well and good, in theory. But Julie was staring at something outside the dome of her pod that made her heart race with excitement.

What if she could never find these creatures again? What if she missed the opportunity just because she was being so precious about Sharman's instructions? Sometimes field work required improvisation and flexibility. This wasn't a lab. You had to go with what you were given.

And Julie could already imagine telling her mother all about it.

"Let's at least get closer," Julie told her pod. She whispered it, even though she could have thought it silently instead. But she liked the old-school way of communicating with her vessel. Like speaking out loud to a dog or a horse. It just felt right.

The pod floated smoothly downward another twenty feet. Julie stared out the domed lid. The material of the dome reacted to her mental desire, even though she didn't express it out loud. The dome honed in on the image, just as if Julie were looking at the black muddy shoreline through binoculars.

Julie smiled. Amazing, simply amazing. A new creature never before seen by a human. She was the first.

There were maybe twenty to twenty-five of them gathered together on the shore of a body of water. The water had a silvery tint to it, like liquid mercury. Maybe it was mercury. She would want to gather a sample at some point to test it.

But for now, all Julie cared about were the small amazing creatures. They were dark brown, maybe even black, and about a foot tall. But that height was deceptive. Their bodies were only about six inches long, upright, with heads shaped like Conquistador helmets: oblong-shaped and tapering up at the top, with one of the skull plates sitting slightly higher than the other. The kind of thing someone making a clay model of the creature might be tempted to shave away to keep the skull looking more symmetrical.

The beings had large round eyes that seemed disproportionate to the size of their faces, but there were no other features that needed to compete for the space. They did not appear to have noses or mouths. Although Julie couldn't be absolutely sure from this distance.

Attached to their short slim torsos were very long, thin arms and legs. Almost spidery-looking. That was the real source of their height. The two sets of appendages grew outward from the sides of the torso, one set on top of the other, with the lower pair about twenty percent longer than the upper. The creatures stood upright on that lower set.

All four appendages looked like they bent in the same two places: at approximately the center and then lower, at what passed for wrists or ankles. The creatures didn't appear to have hands or feet. Just a continuation of the long arms and legs, but bent at the ends the way someone might indicate hands and feet from bending a pipe cleaner.

Because the lower appendages grew outward from the sides of their torsos rather than from the bottom like human legs, the creatures walked with a kind of swagger, like cowboys in the old westerns. As if all of them had ridden all day on barrel-shaped horses.

Their movements seemed slow and awkward. Slightly jerky. As if they weren't sure about where they were about to place their feet. Julie's academic training as a biologist and her many years of experience out in the field in no way prepared her to understand the anatomy of these small creatures. They seemed poorly made. Not at all well thought-out.

But that was always the thrill of getting to know a new species. Understanding over time why they looked and moved and behaved the way they did. Because Nature didn't make mistakes. Everything was the way it was for a reason.

And now it started to make more sense. The creatures were done stepping across the mud at the lip of the shore and were now wading out into the lunar sea.

From what Julie could see from her perch above them, these foot-tall beings needed their long legs to wade through the silver water—or whatever the liquid was—as they appeared to search for something. Food? Wasn't it usually food?

Just the thought of that made Julie wonder if she should grab a snack now while she could. Maybe just a quick bite from her energy bar before … before she did whatever she was about to do. She didn't want to think it yet. She wasn't ready to announce it.

Because the pods had a linked communication system. What Julie thought or said to her pod, Sharman could hear.

Sharman must be busy now with her own survey of the yellow planet. But Julie had no doubt that Sharman kept at least part of her brain on listening for the rest of her team.

Julie didn't have that same ability. Not yet. She could only hear the other pilots if one of them spoke to her directly.

But even that was a miracle in communication. That someone could sit inside their own pod and say something to Julie, and Julie would hear it as clearly as if the person were sitting right next to her.

Julie tried to keep her thoughts down to a whisper. "Closer," she murmured to her pod.

The pod floated lower. And Julie realized she had made a mistake. Because the creatures looked up. Which in itself was a surprise. The material the pods were made of rendered them invisible to most eyes. But the creatures did see her. And they spooked.

And then. Julie was sorry to scare the little creatures, but damn, what they showed her next.

The whole herd of them, all twenty or twenty-five, dropped their forefeet to the ground and took off across the sea.

Now Julie understood the design of their long spindly appendages. The creatures spread their two sets of legs wide out from their now horizontal bodies.

And they skittered across the water. Like insects Julie had watched countless times on streams and lakes back down on Earth. They were called water striders. They could splay out their long legs in such a way that it kept them perfectly balanced on top of the surface tension of the water. And then they could run on top of the water. Run *fast,* just like these guys. The moon creatures were already a quarter mile out to sea by the time Julie was able to process what she was seeing.

And then they were gone. Too far out, maybe, for her to see anymore, or maybe they disappeared underneath the water.

The sea was still. There were no waves or any movement on the surface. As if the creatures might skate across it like solid ice.

But Julie could see from the slight shifting of the edge of it up against the shoreline that the sea was indeed liquid. And it looked thick. Again, reminding her of mercury. And maybe just as deadly if she touched it and let it absorb into her skin.

It was time to call it in. If only to start making a record. Julie had no other way to record her observations than to dictate them to her pod, which meant that Sharman Hix and the others on the team would hear it, too.

"I found something," Julie told them. She made no effort to hide her excitement. With this group, unlike others she'd been part of, no one seemed to give special points for pretending that nothing mattered. Julie described the creatures with as much detail as she could. She reported their behavior, including their escape.

"Has anyone else seen any life forms on the planet?" Sharman Hix asked.

To a person, all of the rest of the team said no.

"Congratulations," Sharman told Julie. "I'd like to see them myself. Locking in to your coordinates."

Julie's special watch buzzed, confirming Sharman's lock on.

"Hold position," Sharman said. "I'm coming up."

The others chimed in. Everyone wanted to travel up to the moon to see.

"Okay, let's meet," Sharman told them. She told the team to lock on to her own coordinates so they could travel as one.

The voices of the team all faded away again. Julie knew it wouldn't take long for them to assemble back into the transport cylinder and then come. For now she was alone in her silent pod, still scanning for any movement down below on the silver sea.

But the movement didn't come from the sea. Instead it came from the edge of the shore. Julie almost missed it, but she caught the quick jerky movement from the corner of her eye. She turned to focus on the spot where she thought she might have seen it.

The pod dome did its part by zeroing in closer. Julie squinted and stared harder. She knew there had to be something there. It wasn't her imagination.

There. So small she would have missed it if it hadn't moved again. If the creature let out any sound, any kind of cry of distress, Julie couldn't hear it. But she had no trouble imagining it.

Maybe the little creature had come late to the shore. Or maybe in the pack's frenzy to get away from the gigantic alien craft above them—Julie knew that must be how they saw her—they had accidentally left this solitary one behind.

It appeared to be stuck somehow. Only one of its legs was moving. Maybe the mud on the shore was thick. Maybe instead of stepping carefully across it, the way the others had, this poor guy had made a mistake and his leg had poked through.

Julie felt a familiar pang. Some of her fellow biologists seemed as cold-blooded as reptiles. They didn't mind watching predators attacking from the air or sneaking into dens or chasing babies and their mothers, trying to separate the two. They didn't mind the killing. The blood and the fear.

But those always bothered Julie. Even though she knew it was the nature of Nature. Even though her specialty was studying predators who lived above eight thousand feet in the mountainous regions of the western US. She had her own reasons for choosing that specialty. And it wasn't because she was immune to the pain, or worse, because she enjoyed the spectacle.

Her colleagues gave her endless grief about it. But Julie was born loving animals, and she couldn't make that part of her personality just go away. She still had to resist the urge to intervene every time she witnessed what was about to be a killing. She knew some people admired the predators for being strong and cunning, but Julie's heart was always with the smaller, weaker prey.

Not exactly the professional detachment needed in a field biologist. It was the same problem she had being among her fellow Marines. Julie joined out of loyalty to her father's father. She admired him for his bravery and his willingness to fight for a cause. She didn't join because she wanted to dominate or kill. She became a Marine to protect others, to fight for those who needed her help.

A noble reason, she sometimes had to console herself, even though it turned out to be dangerously naïve. Her life in the military wasn't at all what she expected it to be. And even though she served honorably, it left scars she could never erase.

But at least Julie's life as a scientist had never let her down.

And now once again she had a decision to make. Or at least an urge to try to squelch if she could.

Julie could still see the strange creature down below in the mud, struggling. If it could only get free, could it run out across the silver sea and be reunited with the rest of its pack?

What would it take, anyway, to free the creature from the mud? Julie was a giant compared to it. It would be like a hand reaching down from the heavens to save a tiny lost being. It would only take a moment. Barely any effort.

The transport cylinder snapped into Julie's airspace. Julie could see through its transparent sides the five other pods all lined up in a row, like gumballs all neat in their dispenser. Sharman Hix's pod was in front. And even though there appeared to be no room for Julie's pod at the moment, she knew the cylinder could lengthen to accommodate as many pods as needed to travel. All Julie had to do was bring her pod to the back of the line, and the transport would expand and take her inside.

Once Sharman assembled the team, all she had to do was tell her pod Julie's coordinates up on the moon, and the transport snapped right to this location in less than the space of a heartbeat.

It was the kind of science that was beyond Julie's comfortable range—and also the kind of science that her mother had always been drawn to. Maybe one day Julie would make herself sit still for more than five minutes so she could apply herself and actually learn it.

But she had the feeling it would take a very long time. Maybe even a year of her most disciplined study wouldn't be enough. And why spend the time on that when there was so much more to learn about the physical world? Julie's mind had always felt better suited to the practical and the observable. Calculations involving space-time and interdimensional travel were outside the boundaries of what she felt naturally curious about trying to understand.

Whereas learning about the biology of another planet and its mysterious moon—*that* was the kind of science Julie wanted.

"One of the creatures was separated from the group," she told Sharman and the rest of the team. Sitting in their transport, the five of them looked like passengers on a train, each in their own spherical compartment with their own individual windows.

Julie pointed down to where the creature still struggled in the mud. She could see Sharman and the others straining to locate the small being. But Julie wasn't waiting for any of them to see it. It wasn't a group decision. Julie was the scientist on the team. This was her call.

Except … maybe she could use another opinion.

"Kirsten? Do you hear anything?"

Julie still didn't quite understand how Kirsten Simmens managed it, but the woman had an uncanny ability to understand languages she had never heard before. Including, Kirsten told her she had realized at some point, the languages of extraterrestrials.

Kirsten tilted her head as if listening. She was somewhere in her forties, with short ash-blonde hair starting to go white at the roots. She, too, had learned late in life to be a pilot, only so she could join Sharman Hix's team and fly pods with the rest of them.

"You're right," Kirsten said. "It's panicking. It's screaming for the others to come."

Hearing Kirsten's confirmation made Julie all the more anxious to get down there and help it.

"Tell it I'm coming," Julie said. But before she could instruct her pod to set down on the black muddy shore, Sharman broke in to stop her.

"What are you doing?" Sharman asked.

"Saving it," Julie said.

"That isn't our role. You know that."

"We can't just leave it there," Julie said.

"Of course we can," Sharman answered. "We're observation only. We're supposed to leave no trace."

"I agree with Julie," Kirsten said. "It's just a juvenile. If you could hear the way it screams—"

Sharman shook her head. "No, and that's final. That's not what we're here to do."

It was what Julie was here to do. She couldn't just ignore the creature's suffering.

She sent a silent instruction to her pod. Just a thought, and the pod responded.

It took Julie down to the surface and set it on the muddy black shore.

"You're making a choice right now," Sharman said. She sounded calm, but Julie could hear the undertone of anger. "That insect, or staying on my team."

It was a threat Julie didn't take lightly. Sharman was right, the rules were clear. They were supposed to make maps and observations, not try to interfere with whatever life they might find on a planet's surface.

"It isn't an insect," Kirsten broke in. "It's small, but it's a conscious being. It could even be highly advanced. It's hard to know because this one is just a baby. I can hear it crying for its mother. It's young, but it's conscious of danger—it's afraid it's going to die. It's screaming out something called the Deeps. If I'm understanding it right."

Julie looked up at where Kirsten sat in her pod inside the transport. She hoped Kirsten could see that she was grateful.

Julie didn't know why she was digging in her heels the way she was. If she hadn't seen the young creature out of the corner of her eye, she wouldn't have cared what happened to any of them.

But she did see. She did know that it was in distress. And Kirsten's information only made it all the more important for Julie to try to help it if she could.

"We're not a rescue team," Sharman said. "We're not supposed to be jetting all over the galaxy looking for aliens to save from rock falls and drowning or whatever else might happen to them on their planets."

"How hard can it be?" Arnie Camper said. He was the sole male on the expedition. Julie didn't know him well. He looked about her age, in his late thirties, with light brown hair he kept in the same short cut he probably got used to during his time flying for the Air Force.

Camper had only joined up with them about a month ago, although from what Julie had heard he and Sharman had known each other for years. He seemed low-key and competent and an easy addition to the team. And his piloting skills were second only to Sharman Hix's. Julie had watched Camper put his pod through maneuvers that looked so incredibly dangerous and also so beautiful, they took her breath away.

The rest of the team were all in their late thirties to early forties. At thirty-three, Sharman was younger than any of them. But she always seemed comfortable in her role as their leader. She certainly wasn't backing down now, no matter who was on Julie's side.

And meanwhile the poor little creature was still struggling to free itself. Julie couldn't watch it anymore. She had to do something.

But she couldn't just pop the lid of her pod and run right out there. The special material of her gray skin-tight flight suit could protect her from head to toe from whatever toxins might be part of this atmosphere, but she needed special head gear to protect her face and allow her to breathe outside the pod.

She reached down into the small pack attached to left

side of the footwell of the pod. Inside it were a few energy bars, a water bottle, some emergency supplies, and a few strips of a strange kind of material Julie had never known existed before she began training for these expeditions.

She unrolled what looked like half a sheet of transparent paper with a gummy surface on one side. It was the gummy surface that was made of the same living material as the pod. Julie pressed one end of it to her forehead. She took a deep breath and exhaled against the material so that it could shape itself to her specific biological needs.

The flat sheet of material began shaping itself around the contours of Julie's face and the back of her head. When she first put on her flight suit this morning she gathered her shoulder-length brown hair back into a low ponytail and pulled the thin hood of the flight suit up over her head. The material that was growing and shaping itself around her took into account the bulge at the back of her hood. Julie had the impression that she could have worn a full brimmed hat under her flight suit, and the material that was growing around her head now would have adapted to that shape instead.

It took less than a minute for the organism to form itself into an air-tight helmet that was tailored just for her. It followed the contours of her face exactly, staying just an inch or two away from her skin. Like the pod, its close fit felt comfortable rather than confining.

Julie took a deep breath. Air flowed within her head gear in the perfect proportion of oxygen and nitrogen as if she were a deep sea diver breathing from a tank. But the head gear did not need any outside source to feed Julie air.

The living material manufactured it on its own. Like her own personal rainforest.

Julie was ready to pop the top of her pod and go rescue the distressed creature, even if it meant Sharman really would drop her from the team. It was a high price to pay, but Julie was committed now. She couldn't imagine turning away and letting the creature die.

And then Arnie Camper's voice spoke inside Julie's pod. Maybe he didn't mean for her to hear, but she couldn't help it. She was connected.

"Come on, Shar," he said quietly. "If it was a cute puppy stuck in the middle of a four-lane, I know you'd want her to save it."

"It isn't the protocol," Sharman said.

Camper cursed in a friendly way, to the effect of forget the stupid protocol.

Julie couldn't see what kind of look the two of them might have exchanged, but the next voice she heard was Sharman's. It sounded tight and slightly annoyed as Sharman barked out her revised order.

"You've got two minutes," she told Julie. "And only because I'm trusting Kirsten."

Julie smiled at the implication that her friend Arnie Camper's opinion had nothing to do with it.

"Open up," Julie asked her pod. The clear dome slid smoothly up and behind her head.

Julie took another breath of oxygen. She crawled out of the pod and stepped onto the lunar shore. It was as muddy as it looked. She felt as if she'd stepped down into a vat of wet concrete. It took her a moment to pull her right foot out high enough to release it from the mud's grip so she could take the next step.

From this close she could see the creature's face clearly. She was wrong about its facial features. She could see that it did, in fact, have a small mouth. That mouth looked contorted in fear and agony. Julie knew that she was the cause of some of it.

She had no desire to make the young creature even more afraid than it already was. She needed to work quickly to free it.

She could only imagine what she looked like to a being who had never seen a human before. She must look like a giant. And an ugly one at that, since her body and face were so completely different from what must pass for beauty among these water striding creatures.

"Kirsten?" Julie said inside her head gear. The team could hear her from here the same as it could from inside her pod. "Anything you can do to help?"

"I'll try to talk to it," Kirsten said, "but no promises. It's still screaming. I'm not sure if I can get it to hear me."

Julie paused a moment in case Kirsten could reassure the young creature of her good intentions. But Julie couldn't wait forever. She had to do what she could.

There were rocks here and there along the shoreline. They looked like black chunks of lava, but weighed much less than Julie expected. She selected one that had a sharp point on one end. She used it to dig a shallow circular trench around the small alien creature.

Then Julie used the same sharp end of the rock to pry up some of the mud. The black mud stuck to her fingers and kept attracting more and more clumps of mud. Soon her hands felt like blocks of wood, they were so heavy and cumbersome.

The little creature continued crying. Julie couldn't hear him, but she could see the open mouth. Kirsten didn't need to translate. Julie knew a look of terror when she saw it.

Finally she was able to free the stuck leg. The little being immediately skittered into the water.

"It's saying the Deeps again," Kirsten said. "I don't know what it means. Except I'm getting an image of the shore where you're standing, Julie."

Julie straightened up from where she had been crouched. She had been careful not to touch either of her knees to the clinging mud. If she knew the sea water was safe she would have tried to rinse the mud off her hands in there. But up this close, the surface looked even more like the thick consistency of mercury.

Her soft black boots felt encased in the wet black mud. She was only a few steps from her pod, but getting there might take some time.

As she strained to lift her left boot free, she could feel a strange vibration moving through both of her feet.

Low, like the feeling of an electric toothbrush just starting up. Julie stood still. She looked around her for the source of the new vibration.

To her right she could see the creature she had freed skittering rapidly across the surface of the silver sea. The sea itself seemed unaffected by any vibration. It looked as smooth as it ever did. The small creature continued fleeing.

The vibration was rising now from Julie's encased feet to the back of her calves. It was time to mention it to the others on the team.

"I'm feeling something," Julie said. "The ground is vibrating—"

Kirsten Simmens broke in. "It's the Deeps. I can hear the others shouting it. They're screaming for the baby to hurry. Julie, you have to get off the shore. Something is very wrong."

The vibration still felt low and insistent, like a constant revolution of a fan. Julie could feel the vibration up her whole legs now, from her feet to her thighs.

"I'm stuck," Julie told them. She could feel her heart starting to race. The vibration wasn't painful, but something about it was creeping into Julie's nerves and making her feel anxious and hyper, with nowhere to dump the excess energy. She still couldn't move. She couldn't free herself from the gripping mud. "I need some help," she said. The vibration moved up her thighs to her hips. Something was wrong, all right, like Kirsten said.

The vibration felt like it was invading Julie's bones. The way hearing a low thrumming bass booming from a car stereo made her feel like even her teeth were starting to rattle.

From where she stood, trapped on shore, Julie could only see the bottom of the transport cylinder up above her. She didn't know what might be happening, but she hoped someone was going to come help her soon.

"Stay here," she heard Sharman tell them.

"I'm coming, too," Camper said.

But Sharman must have gotten her head gear on first because it was only her pod that slipped out through the bottom of the transport and came speeding down to the shore.

Sharman's pod hovered above the mud. The lid slid back into the rim of the base.

"There's a vibration," Julie started to tell her.

"I know," Sharman said. "I can see it."

For the first time since it began, Julie looked up at the surrounding landscape. She had been so focused on her feet, she forgot to check what else might be happening.

Rimming the shoreline were maybe fifty or more hard, rough mounds as big as the kind of snow piles that buried pickup trucks in the winter. They seemed to be made of an aggregate of hardened black mud and the kind of black rocks Julie had used to dig a trench around the trapped young creature.

But the mounds weren't as solid as they looked. The vibration was breaking rocks free and sending them tumbling down to the shore. Julie could feel the vibration in her chest now. It was shaking her living heart. Any moment it might establish a new rhythm that was different from what a human heart required to continue beating.

The low, relentless vibration continued upward into Julie's throat. She tried to swallow it back. But the vibration was too strong.

Julie could feel her brain starting to go under. She was like someone trapped in a flooded room, trying to breathe the last of the air as the water continued rising to the ceiling.

"JULIE!" Sharman shouted. Julie could feel how slowly she turned to the sound. Maybe Sharman had been shouting for a long time. Julie hadn't heard her.

Camper was there now, too, climbing out of his pod into Sharman's, which was closer. Julie didn't know what good it would do. She was about to explode.

She could feel it inside her abdomen. Her guts were starting to turn to jelly. The muscles in her legs were so overcome she wouldn't be able to stand much longer.

Sharman was crawling over the lower face of her pod. Camper was holding onto her legs. Sharman was reaching out.

Julie shook her head. Slowly. It was all too late. She was going to break apart.

Something hit Julie hard in the back. It threw her forward, off her feet. So hard, it pulled her right foot free of its boot.

Julie sprawled across Sharman's pod, arms wide, a single leg free. Then came another crash into her back, pushing her forward and lifting her at the same time.

Her left foot came free of its boot. Sharman dragged Julie into the pod. Camper climbed out into his own, to give them room.

Julie's limbs felt like limp rubber bands. They had no strength or rigidity anymore. She felt like an empty flight suit, hanging over Sharman's arms.

The lid of Sharman's pod came up and over, closing them inside. Then the pod rose, away from the menacing shore. Julie wasn't sure, but she thought she saw her own pod rising, too, trailing them from behind.

In all this time, the sea had never moved. Julie remembered that now. The surface of the silver liquid never vibrated in the slightest.

"They're breaking apart," she heard Camper say. She wondered where he was. "It's all flattened. Are you seeing this? My God."

Julie tried to form words. Her tongue was still feeling the vibration even now. She wondered if the shaking would ever stop.

Her heart didn't feel right. It beat a few too many beats. And not in the right rhythm. It was out of sync.

That was when she passed out. Probably because her heart needed some way to reset itself. And with Julie awake and falling to pieces, how could it?

When the lights came on again, and Julie knew that she was still alive, at least for now, she felt a cold hand pressing against her cheek. Julie tried to open her eyes. Her eyelids felt impossibly heavy. Her tongue was still thick and slow and couldn't form even a single word.

She could smell a kind of acrid, rancid stench. It made her cough to breathe it in.

Her head gear was off. She was breathing in the air supplied by Sharman's pod. But the smell—it was almost unbearable.

The cold hand on her cheek now moved down to rest on her hand. And just that shift stirred the stench up even more.

Julie coughed again. And the smell doubled, even tripled.

It was coming from inside her. The stench was being carried on her breath.

And maybe emanating out through her skin. She didn't smell human anymore. She had done something fundamentally wrong to herself out there on the lunar shore.

Sharman said, "We're almost there." Julie heard her gulp back a breath. Maybe from the stench. It must have been as overpowering for Sharman to smell as it was for Julie.

"Don't die," Sharman whispered, and Julie realized the gulp she heard was Sharman Hix trying not to cry.

Julie tried again to open her eyes. She still couldn't lift them.

She could feel the transport cylinder tilt from horizontal to vertical. They must be back at the Factory already. Thank God for that. The transport must be sliding back through the ceiling of the hangar with Sharman's pod head first.

"Mother," Julie whispered, even though trying to talk hurt her throat and her chest and her mouth. Nothing was working right anymore. Nothing in her body felt like it was lined up the way it should be.

When they started to lift Julie out of Sharman's pod, the pain overcame her again. She passed out. Nature knew exactly what to do.

Julie awoke in the infirmary. This time she could open her eyes. She had no idea if she'd been unconscious for minutes or hours or days.

There were eight beds in the infirmary, but Julie's was the only one in use. She had the long white room to herself.

She could still smell that rancid stench she knew was her own, but at least it wasn't as strong as it had been inside Sharman's pod. Maybe someone had cleaned her up by now.

There were tubes coming into Julie's arms and another into the side of her neck.

Julie tried to lift her arm. She still had very little strength, but at least she could feel that the bones were still in there. The vibration hadn't disintegrated them the way it had the mounds along the shore.

Dr. Caroline Baird smoothed the hair from Julie's forehead. She lifted Julie's left hand and pressed it against her lips.

Mother. They had brought her. Just that small bit of loving contact made Julie's whole body start to relax.

She knew the doctor who was treating her. Dr. Tognocci had patched Julie up before, years before. Her salt and pepper hair was mostly salt now. She looked both relieved and exhausted. Julie's mother looked much the same.

Julie pointed at her mouth. She was thirsty. But she wasn't sure if her mouth would cooperate. Dr. Tognocci pressed a button on the bed. A simple mechanism to make the head of the bed move upward to help the patient sit.

But the vibration—

Julie's body jerked like she'd been electrocuted.

She wanted to vomit. She was certain she would.

Dr. Tognocci instantly realized her mistake. She helped Julie roll onto her side. If Julie was going to vomit, at least she wouldn't choke.

It took a while for her heartbeat to return to normal. Not because of an unnatural rhythm like before, but because of the stress of her body remembering.

Dr. Tognocci and her nurse helped Julie sit up at last. They did it the old-fashioned way, lifting and scooting and stuffing pillows behind her back.

"You will get better," Dr. Tognocci assured her. "The effects will lessen. Here, drink some water. Let's start with that."

Throughout all of it Julie's mother had helped when she could and stepped aside out of the way when she couldn't.

Now she held the straw for Julie to help her take her first sip.

Once her throat was moistened enough, Julie rasped out, "How long? Out?"

"Since yesterday," her mother answered.

Unconscious that many hours wasn't a good sign.

Dr. Tognocci must have seen the look on Julie's face. "I won't lie to you," the doctor said. "You almost died. There's damage to your organs. It's going to take a while for you to recover. But ... I do believe you'll recover."

Julie nodded. She could see tears in her mother's eyes. This wasn't what she wanted to bring back to her mother from the expedition.

Julie had questions for Dr. Tognocci, but forming more words seemed too hard. She might have been asleep for twenty-four hours, but she still felt so tired.

When she woke again her mother and the doctor were gone.

Sharman Hix was there instead.

She sat in the chair beside the bed with her head resting on her dark arms on top of Julie's mattress. She appeared to be asleep.

The only light in the room was a small penlight shining behind the bed. Maybe just enough that the nurse or the doctor could look in on her without waking her up.

By that light Julie could see the threads of gray hair mixed with the black curls on Sharman's head. Maybe Sharman had gained a few more gray hairs after what happened on the moon.

"Hey," Julie whispered. Sharman sat up immediately. Her brown eyes were wide. She looked startled to see Julie awake.

Then Sharman did the same thing Julie's mother did. She lifted Julie's hand to her mouth and kissed it. Sharman smiled in an anguished way.

Then Sharman cursed at her. Julie knew she deserved it. They didn't need to discuss it. Sharman had been absolutely right about all of it.

"The Deeps," Sharman muttered. "Guess we know what that means now. No wonder that little guy was so afraid."

"I should have let him go," Julie said. "Just like you said."

Sharman shrugged. She cleared her throat. She was still gripping Julie's hand.

"You need to write it all up," Sharman said. "I tried to tell your mother as much as I knew, but I was ... busy a lot of the time."

Julie nodded. She wanted to write it up for herself, too. Organize her thoughts. Organize her injured mind.

The weight of what she'd done, all the damage she'd

caused, the danger she'd put Sharman and Camper in—it all came flooding in at once. Julie felt like she might be drowning again. She couldn't take a full breath. Her heart burned inside her chest.

Sharman must have seen the change on her face, because she squeezed Julie's hand and shook her head.

"I've done things, too," Sharman said. "Stupid, foolish things. Someone I loved died because of it. But we're all okay. We survived it. And we learned about that moon. Now we know. So no one will ever make that mistake again."

It was a generous thing to say. Giving Julie an out. But it wasn't enough to say, well, at least we learned.

"I'm sorry for all of it," Julie said. "You won't have to deal with me ever again. I'm quitting the team. Or you already kicked me off. You were right to do it."

"You're not leaving," Sharman said. "Don't be such a coward. I need a scientist. You're not so easy to replace."

Julie leaned back against her pillow and closed her eyes. How she wanted to rewind and go back and do it differently.

"This is how I see it," Sharman said. "If we're the little insects trapped in mud. And we know there's a big bad cataclysm coming for us any minute. Everybody is gone. They left us. They're off somewhere safe already."

"The sea didn't move," Julie said.

"It never moved," Sharman agreed. "They knew what they were doing. Obviously. But you and I are the little one left behind. And we're crying for our mommy. We're screaming for help.

"Then along comes a spaceship from another planet. The alien takes pity on us. It risks its own life to save us.

"Now, I ask you," Sharman said. "In the cosmic scheme of things, don't we want that alien from another planet to help us?"

"Yes," Julie said. She wasn't ready to relax completely. But she could feel some of the tension dropping from her shoulders.

"It's not wrong to be good," Sharman said. "To want to be good to someone else. You screwed up, but I can't say you were wrong."

Julie met her gaze. Sharman held it without looking away. In that shared silent moment, Julie saw a Sharman she never knew.

A young leader. A young woman who had risen to her position over the past fifteen years by working hard and always aiming to excel.

But one who understood how to be true to her convictions. True to her own tender impulses and tender heart.

Julie had known plenty of leaders in her time. Both in the military and when she worked for the government hunting down aliens she was told were a threat to Earth. But few of those leaders were brave enough to show their open hearts. They were too burdened by responsibility or too intoxicated by their power.

"Might take me a while to get back," Julie said.

Sharman let go of her hand and patted Julie's arm. She stood up to go.

Now that Julie could form the words, she needed an

answer to at least one of her questions. Sharman was one of the few people who would know.

"Who hit me from behind?" Julie asked. "When you and Camper were trying to pull me into your pod? Was it Kirsten? Or someone else?"

Sharman chuckled. "I told you before. They have to like you. And yours sure does."

Julie didn't understand. Sharman tilted her head to the side, waiting for Julie to get it.

"My *pod*?" Julie said. "You mean … it did that on its own?"

"First time I've ever seen it," Sharman said. "I didn't know they could do that."

A warmth spread through Julie's veins. A feeling close to sublime. A feeling of connection she didn't realize was possible.

"Like I said," Sharman repeated. "It's not wrong to be good. Your pod obviously knew you were trying to do the right thing. It wanted to help you."

Sharman left Julie with that knowledge as she shut the door of the infirmary behind her. Julie sat in the light from the penlight above her bed and tried to picture what really happened back on that lunar shore.

Her empty pod deciding on its own to try to save Julie from the Deeps. From the relentless vibration that was close to killing her. So the pod decided to push. To bash into her from behind. It freed only one leg, not both. The pod had to try again. Harder, with a thrust upward at the end. That did the trick. Julie's second leg came free, and she was clear for Sharman and Camper to do the rest.

The pod was a living, thinking creature. Just like the small young alien Julie had tried to save.

Not just tried—she *did* save it. She watched the little one skitter off to safety across the silver sea.

And then the chain of saving continued. On to Sharman and Camper. And when they couldn't do it alone, unexpected assistance from Julie's independent-thinking pod.

It's not wrong to be good. To want to be good to someone else.

Julie didn't want to give up trying to take care of those who needed her help.

And maybe here, among these people, doing this strange and other-worldly work, maybe Dr. Julie Trident didn't have to give up anything at all.

THE CANYONS OF A RED DESERT PLAIN

1

M emory was a strange thing. All his life, Arnie Camper had been able to rely on his knife-sharp memory.

But he did not know this place. And he knew he should.

He could feel it in his gut. The displacement. The wrongness of it all. The coordinates were right—he had checked them and rechecked them—but the barren reddish-brown plain beneath his hovering pod, and the deep, darker red canyons cutting huge swaths down the middle of the vast expanse of rock, meant absolutely nothing to Camper's mind.

His memory assured him he had been at these coordinates before, no less than two hours ago. But his eyes were telling him different. No part of this place was familiar.

Camper took the pod up higher. The spherical craft, just large enough to hold a single pilot, responded to

Camper's mental command. The pod was a dark iron-gray on the lower half, with a clear dome on the upper. Camper could see out the dome in every direction.

He wasn't sure what good it was to go up higher. But he had to do something. Maybe seeing the landscape from a greater distance could help him reorient himself. Camper had always been blessed with an innate sense of direction. Even as a little boy, he could help his parents find their way around new cities every time they moved. It was a talent he always took for granted. But now it was as if his brain had blown a fuse. His sense of direction had gone offline, just like his sharp, reliable memory. *Cannot access.*

He didn't like the feeling one bit.

Camper took a breath. Start with what you know. He could puzzle this out if he stayed calm. He had been in far hairier situations before. His whole career with the military, he had flown experimental aircraft that hadn't exactly had the kinks worked out of them yet. That was Camper's job as a test pilot, to find out what speeds and altitudes made the rivets come loose. What made the aircraft go into unintended dives and spirals. What made the landing gear get stuck. And countless other problems large and small that might end up in crashes no pilot could walk away from.

Camper had broken bones. Lost consciousness more times than he could count. He had sustained burns. Had to have his spleen taken out four years ago, when he was thirty-three. By then he had already been contemplating retirement at the rank of Captain, although he sure would have preferred Major. But sometimes ambition had to take a back seat to personal satisfaction. And Camper was personally more than satisfied to work solely for retired Major Fritz Zimholt, the designer and manufacturer Camper had been moonlighting for during most of his career.

There was no question that Major Zimholt's experimental aircraft—the pods like the one Camper flew in now —were superior in every way to even the most advanced military craft.

For one thing, Zimholt's pods were actually alive. Alive and conscious. Independent thinkers. Modeled, from what Camper understood, after some kind of alien tech that had come into Major Zimholt's father's possession back in the 1960s. Camper doubted he would ever find something like that anywhere else but at the Factory, Major Zimholt's underground facility hidden high in the Wasatch Mountain Range outside Salt Lake City, Utah. So he stopped moonlighting and made it his full-time job. He hadn't regretted it for a minute.

His friend Sharman Hix, younger than him by a few years, but, Camper had to admit, a better pilot nonetheless, was in charge of the pilot program. She knew more about the pods and how to communicate with them and fly them than anyone else at the Factory, even Major Zimholt.

And now, over the past year or so, Sharman had been put in charge of the next phase of the pilot program. She was training a select, elite group to start venturing out into space. To explore other planets inside the galaxy. Camper never imagined he might be able to do something like that in his lifetime. The official, government- and military-sponsored space program wasn't even close to getting that far.

But Major Zimholt had others working with him who had access to tech Camper doubted even the most advanced quantum physicists would be discovering any time in the near future. A leap ahead. A giant leap. Camper had made the right choice. He was exactly where he wanted to be.

Except for right now. Staring out through the dome of the pod, surveying a stark red landscape he was sure he had never seen before.

So he was lost. Big deal. It didn't feel great, but it wasn't fatal. He just needed to solve the problem. Start with what you know.

They were out on a day excursion. Another mapping exploration of a new planet. This one was designated Planet C5V-869. Camper was part of a five-member party led by Sharman Hix. Their sixth regular member, Julie Trident, was still out on medical leave. Sharman was using Julie's condition as a constant reminder that they were going to these unknown planets solely to observe and map them. No one was supposed to get involved with any life-forms they might find. Observe and map. Got it.

Even though there were times when Camper—and he was sure the others on the team—wanted to get out and walk and touch and do more than just look.

But that had been Julie Trident's mistake, too. Noted. He had been part of the rescue team with Sharman who pulled Julie off the surface of a moon before it could kill her. He was well aware of the danger.

Although after hearing the full story at the debriefing afterward, Camper was sure he would have handled it completely differently.

Still, he understood that the temptation to get out and get your hands dirty was real. He was the kid who could never sit still in school. He needed to be doing, all the time. Running, playing, jumping, climbing—it was a wonder he ever settled down for pilot's school. But once he decided he wanted to learn to fly, it wasn't as hard as he thought to tamp down the impulse to constantly be on the move. He could sit tight in one place. As long as where he was sitting was the cockpit of some aircraft that he could make climb and soar and zip through the sky.

But at the moment, Camper wasn't moving from this spot. These were the right coordinates. The pod had no controls or indicators, but the team's special watches gave them the kind of constant information they needed. And the coordinates showing on Camper's watch told him the rendezvous was here.

The team had all separated two hours ago to go to their own designated sections on this side of the planet, but it was meant to be just a day excursion. Just the first of many separate trips here. And Sharman was clear, they were all supposed to meet back at their starting point.

So where was everybody?

And more important, where was Camper?

Lost. No matter what his coordinates were telling him.

Two hours ago the team had been together inside their transparent, cylinder-shaped transport ship that held all five of their individual pods in a row.

Below them, at these coordinates—Camper would swear it—was a dark green jungle of massive trees growing so closely together, Camper couldn't see the ground. Ropey vines made of a lighter green tangled among the trees. It all looked wet and humid, even though the air when they first arrived seemed perfectly dry. The jungle continued as far as Camper could see in every direction. This was a jungle planet. Got it.

Sharman said she would map the area directly beneath her. The rest of them were to take off in their designated directions and look for any water sources and make a note of plant life and any other life forms. The pods were invisible to anyone outside the team, and so if there were any life forms, it shouldn't matter. They wouldn't know they were being observed.

But because this place was unknown, Sharman didn't want to risk exploring here more than a few hours at a time. They didn't know the weather here. They didn't know anything about the place. The scientists back at the Factory had been the ones who initially came up with the two-hour limit for the first time visiting a new planet, and Camper had to agree it made some sense. Even if he always hated to leave so soon. His only consolation was that the team would come back again and again and continue exploring. Maybe even tomorrow.

But not if Camper couldn't find the team first. And find the jungle where they all separated just a few hours ago.

He had to forget the coordinates and trust his innate sense of direction instead. And trust his memory of what the place looked like and where he had traveled from there.

Camper told his pod to start back the way they had just come.

They weren't lost, they just weren't in the right place yet.

Camper set out to fix that.

2

The red desert plain continued without relief. The rock looked smooth and generally flat. But there were sections here and there where the rock rose and fell in gentle contours. Camper could imagine running his hand over it to test whether it was warm or cool. The temperature outside the pod was holding at a steady 83 degrees. The sky was a pale greenish-blue. Strange to see. More like water than sky.

After traveling at a steady speed along the route the pod seemed to think they had taken before, the scenery was still the same. No green lush jungle, only smooth red rock.

"Okay, you can stop," Camper told the pod. The pod came to a smooth halt.

Camper checked the coordinates. They were way off. He knew where he was supposed to go, back to where he just left.

There was no point in going further in this direction. Try again.

Camper asked the pod to make a wide circle. Not go straight back, but loop around so he could look.

Time slid by. After the first half hour of searching, Camper asked the pod to speed up the pace. But faster, slower didn't matter. The scenery was all the same.

Another half hour, and Camper had seen enough. By now the team knew he had missed his check in. And yet no one was calling out to him on their comms.

The pods were all connected. First to their pilots with a kind of mental-mechanical bond, and then with the other pilots in the other pods. If Camper wanted to talk to Sharman, he just talked. She should be able to hear him inside her pod, no matter how far away she was.

But he had tried that. He had tried contacting all of them. But none of the team responded. And none of them were calling out to him.

Camper's pulse was steadily increasing. He wasn't afraid, but the whole situation was unnerving at its own level. He had no plan to get abandoned on this planet. And he knew the team would never let that happen.

So it was a problem he knew everyone was working on. He trusted that. He just had to keep doing his part.

And the first rule when you're lost: Don't make it any worse. Don't keep wandering around. Stay put.

"Let's go back," Camper told his pod. The craft changed direction and sped off to the original coordinates.

Then Camper parked it there, high off the red plain,

where he could see the dark red canyons cutting through the rock down to the canyon floor, about fifteen hundred feet below. A sizable canyon. Others he had seen during his recent search looked shallower, but not by much.

At some point, maybe thousands or millions of years ago, a river might have run there. What else could carve the rock like that? But there was no water now. There wasn't a single plant growing anywhere. Wherever the jungle was, it was in some completely different climate. Camper was starting to hate the look of the rock. He had been staring at it too long. And it didn't give him any of the answers he wanted. Where was his team?

The pod began gliding lower. Camper didn't ask it to. But he also didn't try to stop it. He was curious what the pod was doing.

He thought it might land somewhere on the smooth rock. Maybe it was tired of hovering. Camper had no idea if the pods got tired.

But the pod continued gliding past the flat surface of the plain, down into the dark red canyon.

"Hold on," Camper said. "Where are we going?"

The pod continued descending. Not too fast, but at a steady, unbroken pace. No hesitation. It seemed to know what it wanted.

The rock down here looked jagged, rather than smooth. As if huge chunks of it had sheared away. But there were no boulder fields down below to show where they had fallen. Instead, the canyon floor looked as smooth as the red rock up above.

Camper could see he was wrong before. There was water here. A dark, dirty rust color. Not the kind of thing he would dare drink.

It seemed stagnant, even though the red ribbon of it extended across the entire canyon floor. But Camper could see no movement. No swirls, no eddies, no current of any kind. Like a long, thin puddle left after a rain, rather than a stream trickling somewhere to join a larger body of water.

The pod set down on a small flat ledge that sat just above the stream. Camper checked his watch. Temperature was much lower here, only 42 degrees. He couldn't feel it from inside the pod, where everything was always kept in the same, comfortable conditions. He could breathe in here. The temperature was a steady 70 degrees. He wore a specially-made flight suit out of some kind of material Sharman told him was also alien tech, and the suit and its hood kept Camper protected when he did have to leave the pod's habitat. All he needed was the special head gear, made of the same material as the pod, and he could continue breathing regularly no matter what the planet's atmosphere was outside.

He had had to leave his pod to help rescue Julie Trident. The flight suit and head gear had done their job perfectly. All Camper had to think about was getting Julie out of there. He didn't also have to worry about whether he would die from lack of oxygen or from some toxin in the air attacking his skin.

And Camper was getting the feeling now that it might be time to suit up again.

The pod had landed here for a reason.

Camper could talk to it, but it didn't talk to him. He couldn't even ask it yes/no questions. He had to guess. He had to trust. The pod knew they were looking for the rest of the team.

Maybe the pod knew where the other pods were.

Camper had been thirsty for the past hour, but he didn't want to take the time to drink. But since he was leaving the pod, it was time to hydrate and grab some food.

The team kept a small pack full of emergency supplies and a few provisions. These trips were meant to be short. Real food was waiting back at the Factory. Usually after an exploration, Camper treated himself to a big dinner and even dessert. Normally he kept his meals pretty light. Even though he suspected his pod would carry him even if he weighed three hundred pounds, Camper had gotten used to always having to keep his weight down for flying the military's experimental craft. Old habits die hard. It was still hard to relax while eating a piece of pie.

Camper reached into his pack and pulled out the bottle of water and two energy bars. He liked the peanut butter ones. He tore off the edge of the wrapper and dug in.

The meal would only take about three minutes, but he needed to give himself that time. It was no good rushing off without proper fuel in the tank. And Camper wasn't quite ready anyway. He needed a minute. He needed to be sure.

Julie Trident had made a mistake out on the surface of the moon of the planet Oasis. Several mistakes, actually. She hadn't checked the surface before committing. Her boots sank deeply into a concrete-like mud. And she thought she should save a creature who was struggling in that same mud. Camper understood the impulse—he loved animals as much as anyone else—but you can't put yourself in danger doing it. You have to be smart.

Camper wanted to be smart. As he ate his peanut butter energy bars and sipped more of his water, he surveyed the area around him. All of it bare. Just the dark red rocks and the thread of rusty water.

They were in shadows down here. The greenish-blue sky didn't shed its light so far below. Camper could still see without any additional light source, but he had to be careful not to miss something in the low light.

Something like a creature. An alien snake. Whatever was living on this planet. Once you set foot outside the pod, Sharman was always reminding them, you're leaving the safe zone. Get ready.

The pod did something strange Camper had never felt it do before. It rocked from side to side. Like someone tilting a ball from right to left.

"Okay," Camper said. "What are you trying to tell me? Get going? Do something?"

The pod rocked from side to side again.

It was unmistakable. It wasn't Camper's imagination.

"I'm going to put on my head gear," he told it. The pod rocked from side to side. They were communicating, it seemed. Or at least the pod was trying to.

Camper stowed the empty water bottle and the wrappers from his snack back in the backpack. Then he took out the strip of transparent material that would grow into his head gear.

The strip was about the height and width of his whole face. One side of it was smooth, the other was sticky.

Camper stuck the top edge of the sticky side to his forehead. He drew in a breath, then exhaled. From that biological information, the head gear began to create a helmet just for him. It contoured perfectly around the dimensions of his face and the back of his head that was already covered by the flight suit's hood. The head gear created a seal against Camper's shoulders. In less than a minute it was ready. Camper breathed in and out a few times. It was the same as breathing inside the pod. Everything was ready.

"You want me to go outside," Camper said, just to be sure.

The pod rocked from left to right.

"Okay, then open the lid." The clear dome slid back, over Camper's head, and tucked itself into the rim of the bottom half of the sphere.

Camper climbed out. He wore soft black boots with a light tread to them. They weren't meant for hiking and climbing. They were thin so the pilots could keep closer contact with the inside surface of their pods. Sharman even flew barefoot. She said she wanted the closest connection possible.

As soon as Camper was completely out, the pod closed its lid. Camper stood on the rock ledge. He could feel a slight breeze against his flight suit. He checked the temperature again: colder now, only 36 degrees.

He should probably get moving.

But moving ... where?

It all looked the same. Nothing to see here. Certainly no jungle. No people. No pods.

He turned back to his own pod. He had always resisted giving it a name. He didn't know why. As far as he knew, none of the pilots had named their pods. Maybe it didn't feel dignified. But right now, Camper wished he could call his pod by some name. He wished they were better connected. That the pod could tell him exactly what it had in mind.

Camper rested his hand on top of the dome lid. He had pulled out the extra fabric of his flight suit to cover his fingers. No part of his skin was exposed.

He could feel a slight vibration coming from the pod.

But a vibration wasn't enough. It didn't tell him anything.

"So now what?" he asked the pod.

The pod rocked from side to side.

"Okay, I see that," Camper said. "But what do you mean? What am I supposed to do?"

The pod shifted forward on the rock ledge. About half a foot.

"Go that way?" Camper asked it.

The pod shifted forward another half foot.

Camper walked forward, too. There was room on the ledge to stand beside his pod. To his right the red rock wall rose up high, fifteen hundred feet. Its edges were broken and jagged. The rock looked almost black in the low light of the canyon.

And as Camper took another step forward, in the same direction as his pod, he finally heard it.

Heard *them*. Voices. Voices he recognized.

"HELLO?" Camper called out.

"h e r e..." the word came back faintly. Like the people were underwater.

Camper turned toward his right. He tried again. "HELLO?"

"c a m p e r..." The sound was still so faint. But it sounded a little better when he faced this way.

Camper placed his hands against the rough red rock. He leaned forward to bring his head gear close to it. Trying to hear better.

"WHERE ARE YOU?"

"h e r e..."

There must be a cave. Maybe they had fallen into it from somewhere up above. They were trapped down in the well of it. Somewhere on the other side of these rocks.

Camper felt across the wall, searching for any kind of weakness. Some kind of opening. There was none.

He didn't have any tools that could help him dig through. Nothing sharp or heavy. No hammer or pickax.

He had no weapons that could blast it. Really, he had nothing at all.

The breeze blew at him again from his right, from somewhere further up the canyon floor. Camper checked his watch. Temperature 31 degrees. Falling.

What did any of this mean? Where was the team? How was he going to find them and get them out?

Camper didn't know how to get off this planet

without Sharman. He might be out in the open, free, but he was trapped on this planet as much as they were.

This was worst than lost. This was useless. He could hear them and couldn't do a thing to help them.

He felt along the rock again, hoping to find some opening. There was nothing. Not laterally, along the side, not above or below where he heard the voices.

His pod rose a foot off the ground. Then dropped back down again. Then rose again. Then dropped.

Camper couldn't interpret that any better than when his pod rocked from side to side.

"Okay, but what does that mean?" he asked his pod.

The craft rose again, dropped, rose, dropped.

Then it opened its lid. Camper couldn't take that as anything other than an invitation.

"I'm supposed to get inside?"

The pod rocked from side to side.

All of this felt too slow. Camper wanted to do something—now. But how could he, when he didn't know what that thing was? It would be like running around in a circle just to feel movement. It didn't mean he was getting anywhere.

So he climbed back into the pod. The pod shut its lid. Then the pod rose from the rock ledge, fast, straight up from the floor of the canyon.

If Camper didn't know what to do, his pod seemed to think it did. There was no point in trying to interfere. At least one of them had an idea.

The pod continued rising. Out of the canyon, level with

the red desert plain above it. Then still rising. Fast. Up into the greenish-blue sky.

Five hundred feet … a thousand … fifteen hundred … two thousand—

And then the pod stopped. Paused just a flick of a moment.

Then it began hurtling down.

3

C amper had put plenty of jets and other aircraft into rapid, controlled dives. It wasn't the speed that bothered him. It was the destination.

The pod didn't seem to have any intention of stopping. And the desert plain was coming up fast. The pod was going to crash.

Camper knew how to use his own life energy to create a force field around the pod. It was something new Sharman had learned about nine years ago. She taught Camper right away. But it wasn't a natural skill. It wasn't something that came easily to him at all. Nine years later, he was still practicing. He wasn't certain at all that he could do it.

"POD!" he shouted as it continued its manic dive. They were past the smooth surface of the plain now, still hurtling down, aiming for the floor of the canyon.

Camper's food was coming up. He could taste the

peanut butter. Sweat was pouring down his face inside his head gear.

His mind raced along with his heart as he tried to assemble the pieces of the training Sharman had given him. What to think. How to make the force field. How to direct his energy—

But what if it didn't work?

He could see the ugly red water coming closer every second. The pod seemed to be aiming for it, rather than the ledge where it had set down just a short time ago.

"POD!" Camper tried again, but the craft had a mind of its own. Camper braced for impact. He braced his mind. He thought about the force field. But he couldn't feel it—he couldn't make it—it was about to be too late—

The pod slammed through the rust-colored stream. And kept going.

It passed right through it. No barrier at all. Not solid. Maybe even not real.

Because the canyon was gone. The dark red rock was gone.

In its place, down below them, a dense and dark green jungle.

The pod continued diving. Out into sunlight. Into the greenish-blue sky. Camper was above the jungle again, just like he was this morning. This exact spot. He checked the coordinates on his watch. Exactly right.

Where was the team? Where on this planet were they?

And what just happened? What did his pod just do?

It slowed now. The rush was over. It came to a comfortable pause about five hundred feet above the jungle. Just where Camper had parked it a little while ago, waiting for the others to assemble at the rendezvous.

Camper's heart was still pounding. It was still in the dive, still bracing for impact, his mind was still searching for all the ways it was supposed to make a force field.

But it hadn't been necessary. Good. Because if it was, Camper would probably be dead by now.

Although he had heard Sharman tell her beginning pilots plenty of times that the pods weren't suicidal. If they crashed, it was because of the pilot. The pilot had made some mistake.

Camper was fairly certain he had nothing to do with his pod's reckless flight. He hadn't even been communicating with it at the time. The pod just flew.

But its dive wasn't reckless. It was purposeful. Somehow the pod had known how to bring him here. Back to the start. Back to where he meant to be.

"HELLO?" Camper called out. "ANYBODY?"

He strained to hear any voices, however faint.

But all he could hear was the sound of his heartbeat still pounding in his ears.

Camper blew out a breath. He had to get back to an even keel. He needed to think. None of this was making sense.

The pod had brought him through the floor of one landscape, out into the ceiling of this one. But Camper had heard the voices back there, back in the other place. Whatever that place was.

What good could he do them from here?

"Okay," he said to his pod. "I don't understand this at

all. Where are the others? How do we get back to them? And where, exactly, are we?"

He knew there was no point in asking the pod any of those questions. But he had to ask somebody. He had to say the problems out loud. A way of organizing them in his mind.

Camper looked down at the jungle canopy below him. Same as this morning. His memory was clear. He had been right. Sort of.

They had all taken off from here, or someplace that looked like here, and flown in separate directions. Camper had gone off to the left.

Two hours later, he tried to return to this same spot, and found the barren red desert in its place. Down at the bottom of one of the canyons, he could hear the others' voices, trapped somewhere inside the rock.

Then the wild dive into the rusty red stream. Out the bottom, onto the top. And here again, right here.

What was it all supposed to mean?

"How did you know what to do?" he asked his pod. The pod didn't respond. It didn't rock back and forth or move forward or back. It just hovered silently in place.

Camper tried to reconstruct everything that had happened. Tried to decipher how it all fit together. Same coordinates, completely different places. Voices calling to him from inside the rocks...

One landscape stacked on top of another. The pod knew that somehow. The pod had shown him.

How did it know? Maybe Camper would never find that out. Maybe it didn't matter.

What did matter was that Sharman and the rest of the team were trapped somewhere in that other place.

In that other place...

Camper looked down at the dense jungle canopy. From here, it looked impenetrable. But Sharman had told them she was going to map out this area directly beneath these coordinates. They all headed away, she headed down.

Maybe that was the place to start.

"Let's go lower," Camper said. The pod began a smooth and easy descent.

Two hundred feet above the trees, one hundred...

Camper thought he could see a space. A break between the trees where the vines didn't bind them so tightly together.

Had Sharman gone down that way? Was it foolish to try that himself?

Camper's pod had shown him that it understood more than he ever imagined. Sharman talked about the pilots treating the pods as their partners, not as their vehicles. Maybe Camper should open up. Treat the pod like an equal. Just because it couldn't speak in words, that didn't mean it was any less intelligent than a human pilot. For all he knew, the pod was much more advanced than he was.

"Here's what I'm thinking," Camper said. "I think Sharman probably came down this way. Maybe the others came looking for her, and went this way, too. Obviously we need to be careful. Wherever they are, we don't want to end up there, too. But I don't have any better ideas of how to look for them. Do you?"

The pod responded by continuing downward toward the trees.

Just above the canopy, Camper could see a clear cutout among the trees. It went straight down, like a narrow canyon. He checked the coordinates on his watch. They matched the opening to the canyon where his pod had recently hurtled him down to the bottom.

Camper shared that information with his pod. "I don't know what it means," Camper said, "but I feel like it means something. Some kind of parallel world, maybe? Same coordinates, but a different place? Maybe ... some other plane?" He had heard of that from a theoretical physicist he had gotten to know a few years ago. How there might be multiple planes of existence, all in one place. There might be millions of people stacked right up next to us, and we'll never see them and never know.

The pod continued a slow descent through the break between the trees. It threaded the needle cautiously, Camper thought, careful not to touch the trees on either side.

Whether the pod knew something about the trees or not, Camper didn't know. But he thought it was right to try to sneak in silently rather than crashing through them and breaking off branches as they went.

The leaves were the size and shape of watermelons, although they were flat. Bright green vines snaked among them, weaving them together from tree to tree.

But the space where the pod took them down looked like it had been deliberately torn apart. Camper looked at the ragged edges of the leaves. The cuts weren't fresh—he didn't think Sharman or any of the others made them with their pods—but the edges maintained their shapes. The torn ends didn't curl in or look wilted or discolored. As if breaking them apart didn't hurt the leaves at all.

Camper thought he could see how the shapes of the leaves on either side of the break might actually fit together, notch to notch. The way someone finally figured out that the continents on Earth had one time fit together. Like puzzle pieces that had drifted apart.

Camper thought about the rough, jagged edges of the rocks along the walls of the dark red canyon. If he had looked at them more closely, would he have noticed that the walls had been separated and would fit back together, notch to notch?

What did that mean, if they did? What did any of this mean? If Sharman and the rest of the team were trapped in some other dimension or some other world or other plane, how was any of this helping? What was Camper supposed to do?

And what if he was wrong about that anyway? He might be completely off base. Maybe he didn't understand what was going on at all.

The jungle trees were as massive as Camper thought when he saw them from the air. Maybe as tall as the canyon had been deep. Fifteen hundred feet. Could be.

Had Sharman come this way? Camper's pod continued its careful, slow descent. The opening between the trees was just barely wide enough that they continued slipping down through it, all the way to the bottom.

There at the bottom Camper saw something. It made

no sense. At least none that he understood. There was a flat ledge there made of dark red rock. It was even possible it was the same ledge he had stood on down at the bottom of the dark red canyon.

Which meant ... what.

Camper was still wearing his head gear, even though he didn't need it inside his pod. But he hadn't had time to remove it yet with everything else going on.

The combination of gases within the head gear had managed to dry the nervous sweat on Camper's face. He glanced at his watch to see what the temperature was. A balmy 85.

The pod moved forward half a foot. Camper had seen this behavior before. Last time, he had been standing outside the pod on a rock ledge very much like this one, wondering what the pod was trying to tell him through its various movements. He remembered interpreting this one to mean move forward.

But Camper was still inside the pod this time. "Do you want me to get out?"

The pod backed up. So maybe that meant no. Camper said, "I'm not sure what you want."

The pod moved forward again, several inches.

Camper glanced at his watch again.

Thirty-two degrees all of the sudden.

The pod moved backward.

Back up to a warm and tropical 87.

"So it's here," Camper said. "Something is here. Some kind of entrance?"

But if the pod knew, it didn't have time to convey the answer.

Because Camper heard a crack as loud as thunder. Up through the top of the dome he could see darkness closing around them.

The trees began caving in. Branches curled around the open area, curving, clawing at the space, closing around it as tight as a fist.

"Get out!" Camper shouted to the pod, but the trees were on top of them now and all around them. The vines were weaving through the gaps.

It was too late. The trees were burying the pod. Swallowing it into their midst. The last thing Camper saw was the heavy green foliage crowding all over the dome. There was nothing he could do.

He heard the dome of the pod crack.

4

Camper felt like he was drowning. Drowning in a sea of dark green. He could breathe inside his head gear, but what did a crack in the dome mean to the integrity of the pod? Could it still fly? If the trees kept squeezing it, would the rest of the craft start breaking apart?

Camper could feel a vibration inside the pod. He had never felt that before. The pod moved in various ways, but it never vibrated like this.

Maybe it was a sign that the little ship couldn't hold up much longer. It was a living organism, not a machine. The way the trees were smothering it, maybe it was starting to die.

"No!" Camper shouted. "Come on! We have to get away!"

He pushed against the sides of the pod, low where the

interior was a rosy gold, where it felt warm against his touch like it was made of living metal.

And then Camper realized what he could do. He wasn't helpless. He had a way to defend them.

He hadn't needed it while the pod dove straight to the canyon floor, but he needed it now. He had to do it. He couldn't afford to doubt. It had to work.

Camper threw his energy all around the interior. Then he wrapped it outside them, all around the pod. A force field made of his own mental strength. Camper had to close his eyes and concentrate if he any hope of holding it.

He shouted. Shouted to the pod and to himself. Shouted to the trees, "BACK OFF!" Shouted to himself, "DO IT! YOU CAN DO IT!"

He opened his eyes. He was holding his hands outward, pressing against the inside of the dome. He pushed his feet against the foot well. He made himself as big as he could inside the structure.

Sweat was pouring down his face again. He could feel the strain in the muscles of his neck. The effort was mental, but he was matching it physically. Pushing the trees away with everything he had.

The pod was still vibrating. And now that Camper's force field had pushed the trees off the surface, the pod had at least some room to move.

It rocked back and forth, back and forth, each time moving forward a few inches more. And then it found the spot it tried to show Camper before, where the temperature dropped from tropical down to freezing.

And there, pushing forward, rocking forward, the pod found the entrance and slipped on through.

To another plane. Inside the rock.

The appearance was solid mass, and yet Camper and the pod moved through it like it was dark red slushy ice. The same ugly rust red color as the stream at the bottom of the canyon.

The pod continued pushing forward. It was slow going. Like pushing through pudding. But there were no solid obstructions anywhere, just the thickness of whatever it was that surrounded them. Camper couldn't see anything. Just the dark rust red of the liquid rock.

That was what he thought it was, anyway. It was impossible to tell. None of this was anything he had ever experienced. He had no guide for what to do.

The crack in the dome of the pod looked thin and jagged and was about a foot long. But maybe it wasn't really open. Nothing was seeping in from the liquid around them. Maybe it would hold.

Camper realized the pod was lighting the way ahead of them. He didn't realize the pod had lights. Camper had never used them.

They didn't shine like car headlights. They were more of a glow all around the craft. But even with some small source of light, there was very little to see. Everything was the same dull dark red.

And then Camper thought he could see other light ahead. It didn't seem possible. They were so immersed in the liquid rock.

But the pod had been pushing steadily forward, and

now it was true: Camper saw the glow of other lights breaking through the gloom.

Four pods lay suspended in the thick rust-red mush. Camper could see the faces of the team. Sharman Hix, Kirsten Simmens, Nancy Chow, and Frieda Wiles.

They looked exhausted. Frieda looked elated to see him. But Sharman was looking grim.

She shook her head. They were all trapped together now. Camper couldn't save them.

But Sharman didn't know what Camper knew.

"I think I can get us out," he told them. "Just wait."

5

His pod had already shown him the way. How to break through from one plane to the other. The severe dive from a great height, straight down to the bottom of the canyon. No impact, just a breakthrough to the other side.

They would have to duplicate all that force from where they were sitting stuck in the liquid rock.

But they had force they could bring to bear. Five pilots who had been trained how to create force fields around their craft. Camper told them what he had in mind.

Sharman had taught him the theory, at least, although Camper had never tried it. A pilot could share his or her force field with another craft that was in trouble, and protect that craft from crashing.

"We create one unified force field," Camper said. "Sharman, you're better at it than any of us. But if we join with yours—"

He could see her inside her pod. There was light in her eyes again.

"We can still move," Camper said. "My pod has been able to swim through this. Let's get as close together as we can."

Their pods pushed toward each other until the five of them created a cluster, all of them touching.

"Where do we aim?" Sharman asked him. "How do we know where we're supposed to go?"

It was a good question. Camper wasn't sure. But he thought his pod probably knew.

"Which way?" he asked it. "How do we get out?"

It detached from the others and moved a foot sideways to the left.

"That's the wall of the canyon?" Camper asked.

The pod gave a slight rock from side to side. The thickness of the rock was making it hard for the pod to move. But Camper got his answer.

The pod shifted back to the right where it pressed up against the other pods in the group.

Camper explained what to do.

"Sound right?" he asked Sharman.

"What do we have to lose?" she asked.

The five pilots closed their eyes. They began their work.

Camper's sweat had dried, but now a new layer broke out. He could taste the salt inside his head gear.

He tried to concentrate on just the single image in his mind. He tried to create the largest force field that he could.

His pod was vibrating again. But much more than before. Camper looked at the other pilots. He could see the slight vibration in all of their hoods. Their pods seemed to be vibrating, too. It was an all-out effort. All of them working together.

The force field did not start small and expand. It wasn't something Camper could watch as it progressed.

Instead it wasn't there, and then it suddenly was.

Like a ball bearing under pressure, the pods shot out of the liquid rock with such force and velocity, they hit the opposite wall of the dark red canyon.

If not for the force field surrounding them, they all would have crashed and burned right then. But the field made them bounce back and forth like pinballs a few times, until the pods took matters into their own hands and flew straight up and out of the canyon.

The pilots let go of their force fields. Camper slumped back into his seat. He felt twenty pounds lighter. Like he'd run a hundred-mile marathon and hadn't had any food or water the whole way.

Everyone else looked spent, too. He could see the sweat glistening on every face. He was the only one wearing head gear. He would keep it on until one of the mechanics could look at his pod's cracked dome.

Sharman used the sleeve of her flight suit to mop off her face. Camper saw her bend over. She came back with her bottle of water.

The others did the same. Camper had already drunk all of his. But they weren't far from the Factory now. Sharman could get them home just as soon as they all assembled end to end and she could wrap them in the transport cylinder.

For now, Camper took a moment to look down at the landscape below. It was the red desert plain again. The red desert *plane*.

The other plane, where the jungle grew, was somewhere below here, or above it—Camper wasn't sure which.

He would have to describe it all for Sharman and the team later. And then for the scientists. He would be talking for a while.

For now he felt like just resting inside his pod. The pod that had kept him safe. That had ideas and strategies of its own.

He had been treating it like an animal. Like a pet. A horse or a dog. Some kind of airborne companion.

But it was more than that. Sharman was right about calling it a partner. But Camper wondered if even she understood how ingenious the pods were.

It might not be able to speak, but it had a rich and busy mental life. It could plan. It could solve. It could imagine.

Camper had no idea how the pod knew about the passage between the two planes. But that was the only reason he could find the other pilots and the other pods. It was the only reason Camper knew how to save them.

The pod was everything. It had saved them all.

"I wish I knew what I could do for you," Camper said. "Some kind of special reward. But let me just say thank you. You saved all of us."

The other pilots were lining up now. Camper's pod

joined the line. The transport cylinder grew around them. They were one step away from home.

Sharman told the cylinder to take them back. The journey was as quick as the snap of a rubber band. The transport appeared in the mountains just outside the Factory.

Camper was thirsty. He was hungry and he was tired. He needed a hot shower and food and sleep.

But his pod needed care and attention first. It had been injured in the fight with the trees.

When the transport came to rest on the concrete floor of the interior hangar at the Factory, the other pilots climbed out of their pods and let the maintenance crew look them over.

But Camper stayed. "My friend first," he said. "Look at her. That's a battle wound. But she won."

It would take time to fix her. But Camper wasn't leaving.

He took off his head gear and sat down on the floor beside her and settled in to wait as long as it took.

THE SOUNDS OF A CRYSTAL PLANET

1

Kirsten Simmens lay in a heap at the bottom of a scree field. Her right arm throbbed. She had to assume it was broken.

All around her, and up the slope to the narrow path where she had balanced so precariously and had eventually, inevitably fallen, were the pale lavender rocks that looked as small and light-weight as pea gravel, but that weighed more than Kirsten could possibly lift. Like reaching for a grape and discovering it weighed as much as an anvil.

She had seen something down at the bottom of the slope. More than that, she had heard it. And since she was the reason for this expedition to the Planet LX-8H—Planet Lux, someone else on the team had dubbed it—Kirsten felt it was time to justify their faith in her. Because so far, the exploratory team had found nothing. Just this endless landscape of pastel-colored rocks. Lavender here, light greens and blues and pinks in other parts of this planet. No plant life, not even the tiniest scrub brush or weed. No animal life.

And yet … she heard them. Someone. Something. Calling to her, trying to communicate.

Kirsten Simmens had a unique talent. One she had been born with and that her parents first discovered when she was two.

At times, through no effort or intention of her own, she would find herself inside a stream of language passing over her or through her, and she could understand what a person was saying and could answer in their same language. Even if she had never heard that language in her life.

When she was three years old she initiated a conversation in Finnish with an elderly neighbor. How she knew it was his native language, she couldn't explain. There were other demonstrations, other feats of linguistic magic, and she learned to take them in stride. It was just something she could do.

But it wasn't just human language. Kirsten Simmens could also, she discovered, understand the languages of extraterrestrials. She first heard one when she was a child, the call of an extraterrestrial who was lost and trying to find his way home. Her mother thought it was Kirsten's imaginary friend. The fact that "the spaceman," as little Kirsten thought of him, might still be lost and wandering to this day bothered her every time she thought of it.

She tried traditional careers, but eventually people started finding uses for her strange and specific skill. For a time in her late twenties and early thirties, Kirsten lived on a military base as the dedicated translator for three extraterrestrials who had landed their ship there and had stuck around to share some of their very advanced technology.

After that, Kirsten found other top-secret work, acting as a liaison with extraterrestrials trying to communicate with people on Earth.

One step at a time, never knowing where step each might lead, Kirsten had been following a path completely unique to her. There was no guidebook telling her what to do with her particular talent. And though she had mentors, they could only look at her situation from the outside and do their best to advise her what to do next. None of them had ever experienced what Kirsten had, feeling and hearing an alien inside her mind reaching out to make contact, trying to find kindred spirits among the population of what was still a relatively primitive planet filled with a slowly-evolving human race.

And then came this opportunity. To assist in the first exploration out among the planets of a small section of the galaxy.

The technology, experimental though it was, finally made it possible. But the risks were enormous. Although Sharman Hix, the leader of the expeditions, seemed to know what she was doing, it was only within the context of what *could* be known. Like sending out deep-sea divers who knew all about how to manage their equipment, but who knew nothing about the depths they were about to explore. All of it, unknown.

And that was where Kirsten came in. With her strange and unique talent. She was part of the advance team, a two-person trolling team, just her and Sharman Hix. The scientists back at the Factory, where the experimental technology was being developed, came up with a plan and a schedule for exploring just a small sector of the galaxy to start. Then it was up to Kirsten and Sharman to go out and search for planets that might sustain life. Any life. Plant, animal, alien.

Sharman would pilot the transport craft to get Kirsten within listening range. Then, like fishermen using sonar to find fish down deep below, Kirsten would tune her mind into whatever language she might hear coming from that section of stars. Listening for any sign of life.

So far she had found eighteen inhabited planets. The inhabitants were not humanoid, not ancestors of the human race the way some people had theorized. These were species no one had ever seen before. No one had even imagined them, as far as Kirsten knew.

It was the most important work of her life. At the age of forty-seven, Kirsten finally felt she had found her calling. She could barely sleep sometimes, for wanting to get back out there into space and find more. And not just for the thrill of discovery. But because she knew she was helping to build something new.

Helping to build a bridge to other interstellar civilizations. A whole new future of peace and cooperation among the diverse planets and races and species. Humans were not the only living entities in the galaxy. Kirsten was proving that every time she and Sharman went out on a search.

First would be discovery. Mapping and observation. And then, in time, a formal effort to communicate with other planetary species. Kirsten intended to be part of that, too. Even if she was an old, old woman by then, with hair even whiter than it was starting to turn now. Kirsten wanted to offer her special skill for as long as she might live.

The technology that allowed their exploration had come along rapidly over the past several years. The transport craft they used to get them out this far into space was a wonder of comfort and invention. Kirsten had already learned how to fly the single-person pods that nestled within the transport cylinder like little round pills in a pill case. The pods themselves were perfect spheres with the top half made of a clear dome, and the pilots had to learn to communicate with them telepathically. There were no controls within the spheres to make them go in any particular direction or at any particular speed.

But Kirsten was used to communicating with the unknown using the gift of her special mind. Even though she had zero experience flying any aircraft, she learned to pilot the pods within a very short time.

Getting used to flying was a different matter. First, flying above the mountains outside the Factory, a secret facility hidden inside the Wasatch Mountain Range outside Salt Lake City, Utah. And now, more recently, learning to travel out into space without panicking. Kirsten's heart still raced every time she climbed into her pod and lined up behind Sharman's so Sharman could create the transport cylinder around them. Kirsten knew they would be in space in just a matter of minutes. As soon as the transport cleared the ceiling of the Factory's underground hangar, Sharman gave her lead pod the coordinates they were going to explore, and the pod snapped them right to that location in the blink of an eye.

Kirsten pretended she was used to it. That it didn't still scare her every time. But her pod knew what was inside her mind. And it always curled the pilot's chair just a little more gently around her body, as if folding her inside a protective cocoon. Kirsten appreciated the effort. Once her breathing returned to normal, the pod relaxed the chair around her.

Kirsten had visited alien ships before, but only those that came down to Earth and invited humans inside. Her first journey with Sharman out among the stars was almost too much to bear. Too beautiful. Too vast. Too … real. And at the same time it felt like a dream.

But now this was no dream. Kirsten had disobeyed Sharman's order to remain inside her pod while Sharman and the others flew off to explore their assigned territories. Kirsten was supposed to remain in place above this rocky lavender slope and just listen. Direct them to where she thought she heard any noise. Meanwhile the team would observe and map what they saw, even if Kirsten never heard a sound.

But she had heard sounds before. Just a week ago, when she and Sharman first came trolling through this section of the galaxy. That was why the team was here now, on Planet Lux. To find out exactly what might be making the sounds.

The team had already reported in. Sharman wanted everyone in frequent communication after what had gone wrong on their previous expedition.

"Every fifteen minutes," she told the four members of their team. They were still missing Julie Trident, who was out on medical leave.

Because she, too, had left her pod on one of the planets. Kirsten knew she should have learned her lesson from that, but apparently she didn't. Although the truth was, she didn't think much at all before setting foot outside on the rocky planet. Even though she had to take the time to let her head gear mold itself around her head before she asked the pod to raise its lid, it still felt like an impulsive act. One that took a full minute to pursue, rather than only seconds.

Between her oxygen-supplying head gear, and the navy blue flight suit that acted as a second skin around her body, head to foot, Kirsten had faith she would be protected from the planet's elements. And she was. Even as she tripped and began somersaulting down the sharp, rocky scree field, her flight suit kept her skin from ripping. She landed midway down the slope without a scratch on her. Nothing was bleeding.

But the flight suit and helmet could do nothing to save

her bones from breaking. Kirsten cradled her left arm across her chest and supported it with her right hand. She twisted her head to look up back the slope. Her pod was already racing down to get her. Kirsten didn't even have to ask.

But her body was beat up in other ways, not just the broken arm. The pale lavender rocks of this hillside were hard and heavy and sharp. Tumbling down the slope was like being in the ring with a couple of boxers. Even though her pod hovered nearby, waiting for her to get back in—somehow, although right now, Kirsten couldn't imagine how she could do it without losing her balance again and tumbling down the hill even further—she needed time to catch her breath and deal with the pain throughout her body.

Her ribs and her lungs felt battered. Her head was throbbing from being tossed around. She had fallen on her back. The rocks stabbed into her spine. She was alive, she was still breathing, but she wasn't doing well at all.

The pod lined up tightly against the hillside. Its dome lid was still open. Maybe, if Kirsten could get the angle right, she might be able to roll over onto her side and keep rolling right into the pod.

But she didn't trust that maneuver at all. The slope was too steep. And if she misjudged it, she could somersault down the rest of the way, maybe two hundred, three hundred more feet to the pretty green rocks at the base of this hill.

Pretty green, and probably just as hard and sharp as the lavender rocks that were stabbing into Kirsten's back. Another tumble like the one she just took would damage her body even more. She couldn't risk it. She needed help.

"Hey," she gasped. The air still wasn't moving properly inside her lungs. "Anyone."

Normally the team members could communicate with each other simply by speaking inside their pods. Kirsten had never tried to talk to anyone from outside it. But the pod was so close, maybe someone would hear.

Sharman answered right away. "Kirsten? What's wrong?"

Kirsten could only gasp out a few words at a time. So she chose her words carefully.

"Fell ... broke arm ... can't move..."

Sharman's voice seemed to drop a full octave. Her voice of calm authority. Kirsten had heard it before. "We're coming. Hold on." Then Sharman snapped out instructions to the rest of the team.

Kirsten's pod bumped up against the hillside. So close. It was right there. All it would take was just a slight shift in her weight. Off this stabbing hillside. Back into the cushioned pod.

The team was coming. Kirsten just had to wait.

But then her foot slipped off the hillside. And her weight shifted on its own. And Kirsten could feel her body sliding. She tried to grasp something, to somehow arrest the fall, but her hands were useless and her broken arm collapsed as Kirsten began plunging down the rocks.

She caught sight of her pod trying to keep pace with her. Still offering her sanctuary, if she could only fall inside it.

But Kirsten couldn't control anything. Her body was twisting and rolling and tumbling. She cried out in pain. She thought she heard Sharman shouting her name. But it was all a blur now, sight and sound, as she catapulted down the hard, sharp slope.

The last thing Kirsten saw was a bright, vivid light.

Her body continued to plummet. But Kirsten's mind had already passed out.

2

Kirsten had been knocked out before. When she was eight, a girl on the opposing soccer team had rammed into her and sent Kirsten flying up and onto her back. Her head bounced on the flattened grass of the soccer field. Kirsten saw little white stars popping in front of her eyes. Pretty. She would have enjoyed them, if not for the excruciating pain in her head.

She could see pretty white stars like that now, sparkling behind her eyelids.

And she could hear voices, high and soft, not saying words, but making a noise like a beautiful song. Kirsten watched the popping white stars and listened, hoping to understand any of the alien language.

Her respite was brief. Pain slammed back into her body: arm, head, spine, legs, everything hurt her. Nothing was right.

Kirsten gasped and opened her eyes. Her breath still felt

shallow in her battered lungs. She heard herself groan, even though she meant to stay quiet. She wanted to hear the voices, not her own sounds.

She blinked once, again. She was sure her eyes were open. But she could still see the little white stars blinking in front of her eyes. Blinking in the pitch black darkness all around her.

Then it all started coming back. Where was Sharman? Where was everyone else?

Where was the pale lavender slope that had tumbled Kirsten like a clothes dryer? Where was her faithful little pod that kept trying to catch her?

Kirsten breathed in and out as quietly as she could. She still heard the high, beautiful song.

Oh. The answer came popping into her mind. Of course. This was death. The darkness, the sparkling lights, the angelic voices all around.

She relaxed. But she felt disappointed. It was over. She had so much more she wanted to do.

But why was there still pain? Even the slightest movement sent shards of stabbing hurt throughout her whole body.

But what did anyone else know of death? People speculated, even near-death experiencers had their own stories of what it was like, but each person's death must be as personal as their lives. So this was Kirsten's. Absolute darkness, pretty stars, pain, angels singing.

The voices ... even though Kirsten couldn't understand them, she was starting to feel what the sounds might mean.

A question. They were asking her a question.

She answered as simply as she could.

"I hurt."

The song changed pitch and melody. Kirsten couldn't understand it, but she could hear that it was different.

And then she realized what the sound reminded her of. Her seventh grade science teacher, Mrs. Hall, had done an experiment once to show how to make a glass sing. She filled three different wine glasses with different amounts of water, then dipped her finger in the water and ran it over each of the rims.

Kirsten remembered the high, keening sound that rang out from each of the glasses. The pitch of it varied depending on how much water was in the glass. The more the water, the lower the tone.

Running a wet finger over the rims caused a vibration, Mrs. Hall told them. The vibration created a resonant frequency that the human ear could hear. Then she brought out a wine glass made of real crystal. That made the most beautiful sound of all. Kirsten could have listened to it all day.

That was the sound she heard now. Beautiful, eerie, strange. The resonant frequency of crystal.

Kirsten made an effort to sit up. It wasn't easy with her left arm broken. But she couldn't keep lying there. She had to know where she was and what she should do.

But sitting up gave her no more information than she had before. Her surroundings were blacker than black. But piercing the darkness were the pops of tiny white lights. Smaller than fireflies. Easy to miss if the background were made of even a little gray.

"Hello?" Kirsten said. Her voice fell flat. Dampened by the acoustics of this place.

The singing, the music, the vibration from her junior high science class, rose and fell, as if in response. Kirsten tried again.

"Is anyone here?"

The sound rose and the tone lengthened. Like someone holding a note on their instrument.

If this was someone's language, Kirsten couldn't understand it. It was the first time she felt completely cut off from her special gift.

But maybe that meant that this wasn't a language at all. These were just sounds. Not meant to be interpreted as anything approaching words.

But ... maybe they were for something else.

Nearly twenty years ago, the three extraterrestrials Kirsten had acted as interpreter for had one day suddenly disappeared from the military base.

They left their spaceship behind. No one knew how they got away.

But one person knew. Reggie Swann, the designer and mechanic who had befriended the three ETs and spent seven years learning everything they wanted to teach him.

Kirsten and Reggie were friends, too, but not close enough back then for him to reveal the secret to her of how they escaped.

When he finally did tell her, it was with one word: *resonance.* That was what RayJay, one of the extraterrestrials, had called it.

The ETs created a vibration inside their craft by

striking metal spoons against the inner walls. They used that vibration—that resonance—to return to their home planet. They didn't have to travel through distance over however many light years a more primitive spaceship would have to travel. They had used the resonance to slip through to their own dimension.

Reggie had used that same resonance to leave Earth to visit them. And he returned to Earth with a more complete understanding of how to build spacecraft with technology that incorporated what he learned from the ETs.

It was why the transport cylinder could arrive at its destination in the blink of an eye. Reggie Swann had come back to the Factory to upgrade the pods he had originally designed, this time giving them the technology that allowed them to travel in space and return to Earth the same day.

Resonance.

Not a language, but a method. A technology. A cause and effect.

The sounds caused an effect. But what effect, exactly?

Kirsten sat in the darkness watching the sparkling white lights. She cradled her aching broken arm in her right hand. She could breathe easier now. She hoped it meant her ribs were only bashed, not broken. Everything still hurt, including her head.

But at least she could think clearly. And she needed to right now. She wanted to remember everything that had happened.

The lavender scree field. The rocks looked like they should be loose and lightweight, but they were so heavy it was almost as if they were glued to the steep slope. Even though Kirsten came plummeting down the hill, the rocks didn't tumble with her.

She should probably be grateful for that. If one of them fell on her, who knows how many more bones might have broken.

Why had she lost her balance and fallen in the first place? That was harder to remember. She had heard something down at the base of the slope. Why didn't she just fly her pod down there to look? Why did she put on her head gear and climb out?

She couldn't remember the reason. Sitting here now, it didn't make sense. She knew the danger of leaving her pod while she was alone. So why did she take that risk?

And then, once she was lying midway down the slope, how did she lose her balance again and start falling the second time?

She had been careful not to move. Even though she considered rolling toward her pod. But she was too afraid. She thought she had been careful not to move even a finger.

But then her leg shifted and she was falling again.

When everything about the hillside seemed completely solid. She could understand it if the loose rocks had shifted and taken her with them. But that wasn't what happened. Kirsten was sure of it.

But there was something. A sound. Not like the high tones she could hear now in the dark. A sound that was lower, that might have been short and sharp. And then her leg slipped and she lost control.

Then she had heard Sharman somewhere close by. Maybe the whole team was there to help. So what happened to all of them? How long ago was that? How long had Kirsten been unconscious?

"I have to get back to my friends," she said.

And the sounds that answered her were beautiful and soothing.

Like the music from the rim of the crystal wine glass, but longer, more sustained, and rising and falling as if there were more water in the wine glass, then less, then more.

And then a new light appeared. And even though it lasted only a moment, Kirsten could now see where she was.

It seemed to be a small cave. In the flash of light she could see the sloped walls around her. The space was about double the size of one of the pods. Enough for two pilots to sit inside, not just one. High enough overhead that Kirsten could stand if she wanted. And though the air felt slightly colder than what it was on the scree slope, it wasn't uncomfortable. She wasn't shivering.

Kirsten breathed out and breathed in the mixture of oxygen and other gases inside her head gear. She was relieved to the know the long, hard fall hadn't compromised the helmet. So she could survive here in this dark cave, at least for now. But she still had no idea how she got here or where it was.

She waited for the light that had briefly flashed to reappear. But once again she sat in pitch black darkness with the little pops of tiny white light.

She didn't understand the language of the sounds she was hearing on this planet, but she knew how to make her way toward communication. Just repeat what worked.

"I have to get back to my friends," she said again.

Again, she saw the light.

This time she knew where to look before it appeared. So even though it only lit briefly, she captured a good glimpse.

It was shaped like two halves of an acorn squash opened wide, but still joined at the back seam as if someone hadn't cut completely through it. Each half looked dark blue inside. In the middle of each was an orange ring around a yellow light that momentarily glowed.

The orange and yellow centers looked a little like fish eyes. But they looked hard, more like rocks than flesh.

Kirsten realized the next moment what the image reminded her of: a stone geode that looked rough and dull on the outside, but once you broke it open, there was a beautiful colored crystal inside.

Her father used to have a small geode on his desk that he used as a paperweight. Kirsten used to examine all the intricate crystal patterns inside whenever she was bored and waiting for him to finish work.

It was time to try a new sentence. See if she got a different result.

"I need help. Can you help me?"

That lit up several geodes on the wall. In front of her, dark red. To the left, a clear white. To her right, a pale blue.

Kirsten was getting somewhere. She just didn't know how to interpret any of it.

"I need help. I have to find my friends."

Red, green, white, light blue, lavender.

She could go on like this all day. She wasn't getting anywhere.

And it was frustrating not to hear any language inside her mind. The gift she had relied on all her life wasn't working here.

Except ... maybe she just wasn't listening for the right thing. She was listening for sounds. But what if this language was made of color?

"I..." Kirsten said, then waited.

"I," she said again.

Low on the wall, to her right, a pale green light glowed for a moment and then went dark.

Kirsten repeated the image of that color in her mind.

The light green geode glowed on the wall again.

Communication. Okay. It was possible.

Time to build a vocabulary.

Word by word. Color by color. Until Kirsten felt she had enough to build a few sentences. Not only to speak in this cave's language, but to understand if it tried to answer.

The beautiful, eerie sounds she heard before were gone for now. The cave was silent except for the sound of Kirsten's legs shifting against the light dirt on the hard rock floor. She could hear her own breathing inside her head gear, but she doubted anyone or anything in the cave could hear it.

And what was she dealing with, exactly? Were the

inhabitants of this planet rocks, rather than plants and animals?

Is that why the team had seen so many different colored rocks in different sections of the planet as they first flew over it? Were those the equivalent of different towns or territories or however stones would divide up their world?

And what was this cave? Was it a building within a town? Kirsten was so used to translating and interpreting, trying to communicate in an alien language, but her usual methods weren't working for her now. Maybe she should stop trying to compare and contrast. Just take this place for what it was. The point was exploration. Discovery. She was discovering, all right.

But now she felt tired. Hungry. Thirsty. Everything in her body still hurt. She was tired of sitting in this position, in the middle of the cave floor. She cradled her broken arm against her chest and began scooting back to lean against the cave wall. Just for some support. Just to rest.

Not expecting what would happen next.

3

Now there were more than tiny pinpricks of white lights.

Kirsten floated in a field of stars.

Panic rose in her chest, it clogged in her throat. This was worse than her first time flying into space in the transport cylinder. At least with that, Sharman was in the front, piloting, and Kirsten just had to sit inside her pod and watch space all around her outside.

There was no outside now. Kirsten was *in* it. As immersed as if she had fallen overboard from an ocean liner and now floated in the sea all alone.

The air—the space—had weight to it. She could feel it gathered around her. Like a thick fluid she could see move when she moved her arms.

Her arms—

They were both extended from her body, floating in the

ROBIN BRANDE

thick darkness of space. And her left arm was fine. It wasn't broken anymore.

In fact, her whole body felt fine. Even refreshed. Kirsten looked at her arms, her hands, her legs and feet. All of them still encased in her navy blue flight suit. She still had her soft black boots on. She felt her face. The head gear was still intact.

If she really was floating, suspended in this thick air or fluid or whatever it is, then maybe she should just lie back and let it hold her. She tried that. She felt better.

Cocooned the way she felt supported by the pilot's chair inside her pod. But this was even better because she truly could relax.

Despite her initial panic, she wasn't afraid anymore the way she usually was out in space. She wasn't sure why. But she could feel that the weight of her fear was gone.

Kirsten lay still for a time, just concentrating on her breath. In, out, in. There was an almost aluminum scent to her breath inside the helmet for some reason. Faintly metallic, but not unpleasant.

There was nothing that had to be done. Nothing she could do. And that gave her freedom to think without pressure.

There was no timetable. She didn't have to figure anything out. She could just look around her and notice where she was.

The darkness was not as absolute as it was inside the cave. And it didn't have boundaries like the cave walls.

The lights here were larger, the size of lemons and

cantaloupes, and they glowed with those same colors, lemon yellow and cantaloup orange.

Just thinking of food colors should have made her hungry again, but Kirsten felt no bodily needs at all. She wasn't tired or hungry or thirsty anymore. Nothing hurt. Everything was actually fine.

Even knowing she had somehow slipped into this separate dimension felt fine. Even knowing she might be stuck here forever didn't make her afraid.

Because Kirsten knew what this was. Reggie Swann had described it years ago. First, the way he had watched RayJay and the other two extraterrestrials slip behind some divide, like they had shifted aside a curtain.

They disappeared from the dimension that Reggie Swann and Kirsten Simmens lived in. The ETs returned to their own planet and own dimension someplace else.

When Reggie finally figured out how to go visit them, he traveled inter-dimensionally, too. He described to Kirsten what he saw when he left: a field of black matter, lit by bright yellow and orange stars.

So if that was where she was, Kirsten didn't have to panic. She just had to find a way to return to her old dimension.

Reggie Swann knew how to do it, but he never shared the details with Kirsten. It wasn't necessary. She was never going to travel the way he did.

She liked the way she and Sharman and rest of the team explored the galaxy. Reggie had to travel alone. That wasn't how Kirsten wanted it.

But whether she wanted it that way or not, here she was, alone.

Floating on dark matter, lit by yellow and orange stars.

If this was the same place where Reggie went, then maybe Kirsten could go as far as he did.

There was only one way to know.

Kirsten reached out with her mind.

She still knew the language she had spoken with RayJay and Linus and Mit, the three extraterrestrials she had lived with on the base all those years ago.

Their language felt like a spiral in her mind. She loved the way it looked and sounded and felt. It was all telepathy. Her mind loved to hear it and answer.

Kirsten wasn't lost, she just wasn't where she meant to be. But she wasn't alone if she could find her old friends.

The line of stars sharpened. They were no longer in random-seeming clusters and points. They lined up in front of her, yellow and pale orange stacked one on top of the other.

On one side of the line Kirsten floated in a sea of black. On the other side of the line the darkness was growing lighter and lighter by the second.

Kirsten reached out her left arm. It still felt whole and healed. She spread her fingers. She could almost touch the divide.

But she was still an inch or two short. So she kicked herself forward with her legs. She reached again. She could grip the edge of the line of the stacked stars.

"RayJay!" she called with her mind, and she could hear her old friend calling her back.

Kirsten got both hands on the divide and pulled herself to it.

All it would take was a twist of her body, and she could roll over to the other side.

Once again she heard the high musical voice of vibrating crystal.

Kirsten hesitated on the brink.

Because she knew what that sound was.

It was coming from behind her, from the dimension she was leaving behind.

The crystal planet was back there. Her life, her work, her friends were there.

But knowledge was in front of her. She could pull herself right to it.

She didn't have to wonder what other planets and intelligent life were out there to be found. She had already found extraterrestrials years ago and befriended them.

And there had been other ETs since then, others Kirsten had communicated with and learned from. She had been searching for this kind of knowledge for all of her life.

Ever since her "spaceman" had called out to her when she was just a little girl, sitting at her family's kitchen table, coloring a purple elephant.

Now Kirsten was the one floating someplace unknown. She was the one calling out to a being from another planet who she hoped could hear her.

But the spaceman from her childhood hadn't asked for help coming to Earth. The spaceman wanted to return to his own planet and his family.

Even if Kirsten knew how then, it wouldn't have been right to bring the spaceman to her house instead. He was an explorer who wanted to return home.

Kirsten still gripped the edge of the star-filled divide. She could feel the vibration of the lemon-colored star in her right hand.

"Oh, RayJay," she thought, and she sent a feeling of great love along with her words. "I still miss you and Mit and Linus. I hope you're all well."

But their world wasn't her world. Not as a place to stay. A place to visit some day, yes, she would love that.

Reggie Swann had stayed with them for years, but Kirsten wasn't ready to do that herself.

She had friends. A life. A calling.

"Please help me get back," she asked RayJay. She could feel him on the other side. Kirsten didn't know how to move in this dimension, but he did.

She could see an image of the extraterrestrial in her mind. RayJay's mouth was too small to curve into a smile, but she could feel his happiness that she had come so close to where he lived.

"Turn," she heard him say inside her mind, speaking in her own voice, the way he and the other ETs did.

Kirsten let go of the line of stars. They dispersed again, to where they were before. Kirsten couldn't see the divide anymore. Now there was nothing but darkness and the sparkling yellow and orange lights.

"Turn," RayJay told her again.

Kirsten rolled to her right and faced what felt like a different direction.

Then from behind her came a ringing, like a metal spoon striking the inside of a metal ship. RayJay was supplying the vibration so Kirsten could return. She could hear the ringing behind her, and now also a ringing before her.

The sound in front was growing louder and louder. If there was still ringing behind her, she couldn't hear it anymore.

A new divide appeared in the blackness. Kirsten could see it by the light of a thousand sparkling white stars all lined up in front of her. She reached out with both hands to grip the edge and she pulled herself forward.

She swam through the darkness into what seemed like an underwater cave. There were beautifully-colored crystals glowing along the walls.

By the light of a silver crystal Kirsten could see what she hadn't seen before. There was a small opening in the cave wall. A current in the black matter around her was pulling her toward it. Kirsten aimed her arms forward and let the current take her.

She didn't know if she was underwater or just encased in dark matter like when she floated out in space. But her head gear allowed her to breathe. Her flight suit protected her skin. Whatever surrounded her continued pulling her forward through what felt like a tunnel.

The lights were gone. Everything was black. But Kirsten could still feel herself moving through.

The silence was as thick as the substance around her. There were no sounds of ringing or high singing or RayJay talking inside her mind in her own voice. Kirsten had never experienced silence so absolute.

And then with one big push from the current, she was out of the tunnel and back on the hillside. The pale lavender rocks were stabbing her in the spine once more.

Kirsten's pod hovered beside her, bumping against the slope. It wanted her to roll, to move so it could catch her.

Kirsten felt no fear. That was new for her. But she knew what it felt like to be fearless floating in space, and having experienced it once, she wanted to feel it again.

So without hesitation she did what her pod wanted. She tucked her arms against her side and rolled to her left.

The pod scooped her up. Kirsten fell awkwardly down into the belly of her pod and sprawled on top of her pilot's chair. But it only took a moment to push herself upright again, using her two equally healthy arms.

Her head no longer throbbed. She could breathe easily again. She sat in the pilot seat and let the pod close its dome over her head.

Sharman and the others were nowhere near. Maybe Kirsten hadn't called to them yet. Maybe she had come back here at an earlier time.

Or maybe, since her arm wasn't broken anymore, she had come back to a different timeline altogether.

Reggie had told her of such things. And Kirsten had seen miraculous things herself. Years of communicating with extraterrestrials had shown her that her education about time and space had been plain wrong.

It meant there was more to know. More to explore. Kirsten could spend her whole lifetime discovering more.

"Let's go find the others," Kirsten told her pod. It took off smoothly at an angle. It flew over the sharp steep hillside made of pretty lavender rocks.

There was a cave somewhere down at the base of it, lit by beautiful crystals. There was a tunnel that led either to it or from it.

But Kirsten didn't need to find it again. In fact, she would tell the others about it, but warn them not to look for it.

Because if not for her friendship with RayJay, she might never have found a way out of the dimension where the cave took her.

Maybe someone else on the team wouldn't have minded disappearing forever. Reggie Swann told her that when he left he hadn't planned to ever come back.

There were tricks to getting around, out and back and forward and back in time and space, but Kirsten didn't know them yet and might never know.

She could see a pod in the distance. One of the team members doing their work.

This was Kirsten's work, too, helping them explore, helping them find the places where life might exist.

The life here was crystals. A language Kirsten didn't speak.

But she had done all right. Not perfect, but all right. And unlike RayJay, Kirsten's mouth was wide enough that the edges of it could turn up into a smile as her pod hurried her back to her people.

THE GLASS MOUNTAINS
OF AN ICE PLANET

THE GLASS MOUNTAINS OF AN
ICE PLANET

F rieda Wiles felt out of place. She was out of place. On a distant planet.

And the fact that the planet was covered in ice shouldn't unnerve her. She had been in plenty of icy conditions before. She even spent a month at the McMurdo Station on Antarctica, participating in a special research mission when she was in the Navy.

The temperatures there sometimes got as low as minus sixty degrees. So she knew ice. She knew cold.

But this was different.

The sky was a dark charcoal gray. But not because of clouds or an incoming storm. The sky looked clear. This was just the color. Gray as unpolished lead.

The land below, visible through the clear dome of her single-seater spherical pod, wasn't pure ice and snow like it was at the South Pole on Earth. Instead, it looked flat and dry, almost dusty, and as gray as the sky above it. There were bluish-silver ice mountains rising from the surface, maybe as high as four or five thousand feet.

And here and there, dotting the landscape, were large round balls of bluish-white ice, as big as sedans, that looked like they might have rolled there from some unknown location. They didn't appear to have come down the mountains. How could they? The mountains were as solid and smooth as glass. It didn't look like anything had broken off them in centuries—or possibly ever. There wasn't a single crack or chip or flaw anywhere Frieda could see.

She looked again at her special watch. It gave Frieda the coordinates of where she was, and also information like wind speed and temperature.

There was no wind. Zero. And the temperature was minus twenty-two.

Her pod hovered in place, maybe waiting for her to make a decision.

"Let's go look at that mountain," she told it, pointing to the smaller one that was closest. Another mountain rose high behind it. Frieda felt intimidated by how massive and strange it looked. She knew that other planets wouldn't necessarily look anything like Earth—and she had already seen several that were absolutely strange—but something about this place just made her blood run cold. And not because of the temperature.

She was thirty-five, an ex-pilot with the Navy, shorter than she liked, a little plumper than she liked, red hair a little too untamed, but otherwise she was generally confident in her appearance and her behavior and her skills.

Frieda liked order. She liked predictability. But despite that, no one would accuse her of being rigid. If she liked her life organized, it was so she could feel free to improvise whenever she needed to.

Even now, in her civilian life, she kept a duffel packed at all times and sitting by the door of her room at the Factory. She could be ready to go, ready to rise to any emergency, at a moment's notice.

She never understood her fellow aviators who had to scramble to get ready. Why not take that worry off of your mind? Frieda used to lay out her clothes for the next day when she was a little girl going to school, and she still did that as an adult. Why not? It made everything so much easier.

Frieda checked her watch again. She was wasting time. For what? Just a strange feeling. And while she trusted her instincts—they had saved her more times than she could count during her many years as a pilot—she knew there was such a thing as superstition. Not a hunch. Just a weird feeling that didn't necessarily mean anything. Maybe this was one of those times. Maybe the gray sky was throwing her off, triggering a feeling of dread. Like some kind of seasonal sadness.

The other four members of the team were out exploring different sections of the planet. From what Frieda had heard during the past two check-ins, everyone else was seeing pretty much the same things she was.

Arnie Camper found a dark blue river that cut through the flat gray surface ice, but that was about it. Everywhere else seemed to be just glassy silver-blue mountains and these weird balls of ice.

Frieda's pod glided closer to the top of the nearer mountain. Frieda stared down at the slope. She was wrong before, it wasn't entirely smooth. There were channels formed down the length of it, the way a glass blower might create folds in a decorative vase.

If there were water up here, a lake, for instance, then it would make sense that the channels were dug out by years of flow. But it was all as dry up here as at the base of the mountain. The geology operated by different rules than on Earth. Maybe ice just pushed out of the surface and rose upward over eons, and now these mountains stood stark and perfect above the landscape, too cold to melt, too hard and steep to scale, and no life could ever make it here after all.

But the reason they had come to Ice Planet 2, as they were calling it (Ice Planet 1 had been as off-putting, but in different ways), was that one of the team members, Kirsten Simmens, had heard or at least somehow sensed that there was life here.

Frieda knew by now that "life" could be anything. Crystals. Insects. Plant life. A jungle that might try to swallow you. Water striders that knew how to escape the dangers of land. Creatures of the air that didn't take kindly to human-piloted pods crowding into their space. All of them different from anything Frieda had ever seen for herself or watched on a nature show. But that was the point of exploration, wasn't it? To see, to learn, to know.

So she wasn't giving up, even though everything

around her looked frozen and lifeless. That wasn't her call. Her role was to survey the area, observe what she could find, report in to help the team leader, Sharman Hix, decide whether to concentrate the team's efforts here or someplace else.

They were checking in every fifteen minutes now. Too much could happen in fifteen minutes. Sharman insisted now they all keep in closer contact.

Frieda heard her fellow team members sounding off.

"Still following the river," said Arnie Camper. "See how far it goes."

"I'm stationary," said Kirsten Simmens, their extraterrestrial interpreter. "I'm listening. Still don't hear anything. Not like before."

Kirsten had come out on a scouting mission with Sharman the week before to listen for any sign of intelligent—or even primitive—life on the planets in this sector. Ice Planet 2 gave her some kind of hit last week, but maybe that was a fluke. Or maybe the intelligent life proved its intelligence by getting off this gray, depressing planet.

"Nothing," Frieda said. "Just looking at one of the glass mountains more closely. But I don't see anything living anywhere."

"Same here," said Sharman Hix. Frieda could hear her sigh. The voices of each of the team members came through loud and clear into everyone's pod, just as if the person was sitting beside each individual pilot.

There was a slight pause. Routine. But ... then the pause went on.

"Nancy?" Sharman asked. The fourth team member,

Nancy Chow, around Frieda's same age, but not at all like her either physically or by temperament, still hadn't checked in.

Frieda had trained on the pods with Nancy. She liked her. They had the same world view. But there was no question that if someone was looking for a classic flier, Nancy Chow was it. Ex-Air Force, a small, wiry body, better eyesight than a hawk's, a serious no-nonsense expression that could suddenly break into a huge smile that would throw off anyone who didn't know her. She was fun. A lot of fun. She flew with a kind of joy Frieda just couldn't capture. Frieda was always too much in her head. She knew it. Nancy Chow just seemed to have been born with both a sharp mind and a light heart.

"Nancy," Sharman said again.

And this time Frieda could hear her friend's excited voice. "Guys." Nancy Chow laughed. "Oh boy. You won't believe it. Come over to me. I have to show you."

Frieda was relieved there wasn't a problem. The team had already had one too many scrapes. Nancy read out her coordinates and Frieda asked her pod to take her there. They flew over the gray ice, a safe distance above the car-sized ice balls down below, and now Frieda could see them more clearly.

They were perfectly smooth and round. Even more perfect than the glass mountains. They rested on the gray surface ice looking solidly in place, but their bottoms weren't flat in any way. A stiff wind, or another ball rolling right up against it, and the ice ball had no reason to stay put. Who's to say these balls didn't roll all over the planet, staying in one place just a day or two before moving on to a new destination?

"Higher," Frieda told her pod. She didn't like the look of those ice balls at all. They were the same spherical shape as her pod, but much larger. Not just car-sized, but house-sized. Frieda had no desire to get in any of their way.

She liked to think she was a lot tougher than this, not jumpy, not superstitious, but damn, this place made her nervous. Why? It was just cold and gray—so what? But it was like peering into a dark well and not knowing how deep the thing went. It made her feel uneasy. Unanchored. Like she might fall and never come back to ground.

Up ahead she could see the gathering of the other pods. That brought her instant relief. Maybe she just didn't like being alone in this place. Being with the others felt almost normal again.

"You're going to have to magnify," Nancy told them. She gave a nod to the clear half dome on top of her pod.

Sometimes the pods acted on their own, zooming in on the landscape or some feature they knew the pilots wanted to observe more closely, and sometimes it was up to the pilots to ask.

Frieda's pod didn't wait for her to ask. At Nancy's suggestion, it began focusing tighter and tighter on the glass mountain they were all hovering near.

It looked exactly like the one Frieda had observed just a few minutes ago. The same smooth, flawless surface, but with gentle, artistic folds in it. It looked like it had been designed, not just formed by years and the elements. It was too perfect. Too decorative. But maybe all the mountains on this planet were that way.

Nancy pointed to a spot on the left side of the smooth glass slope. Now that Frieda's pod had zoomed in on it, Frieda could see what Nancy had noticed.

There was a small round feature there that looked out of place with the rest of the mountain. A flaw, if you wanted to call it that. Something that broke up the perfect line of the smooth glassy slope.

A round ball about the size of a baseball. Barely visible without magnification. The rest of the mountain was so huge—maybe ten thousand feet tall—a little baseball-sized pimple could hardly draw the eye.

"You have to look really, really closely," Nancy Chow said. Then she chuckled again. Frieda shot her a glance. What on Planet Ice 2 could possibly be so funny? But then Arnie Camper said, "Whoa."

"Magnify, please," Frieda politely asked her pod.

The dome zoomed in closer. Then closer again. Frieda's eyes adjusted to the new scene.

There was a little crew, if you could call it that, massed up on top of the ice ball. Frieda counted six beings, barely visible against the silver-blue ice of the mountain and the bluer ice of the baseball.

They were wedge-shaped. Not humanoid at all. They didn't look like any animal Frieda had ever seen. They had no arms or legs. But they did have mouths.

And now Frieda thought she saw what made Nancy Chow laugh.

The six wedge-shaped beings were silvery-blue like the

glassy mountain. But their mouths were a darker color. Almost black, maybe closer to charcoal, like the sky. Their mouths were just straight lines across the width of the narrow tops of the wedge. And out of their mouths were coming a steady stream of ... spit.

Frieda gaped at what she was seeing. With the magnification, she could watch it fairly closely. The six wedge creatures would dribble out a unified stream of dark blue spit—dark blue, maybe, like the river Camper had been following—and the ice ball would get slightly bigger. Then they would wedge it down the slope maybe an inch or two. Then more spit would dribble out, the ball would get slightly larger...

How long must it take them to build something as large as the ice balls Frieda had seen down below?

Was that what she was watching? Were the creatures creating something that would eventually race down the slope and land on the gray surface ice?

Why on earth? Why on Planet Ice 2? It looked like the most laborious, useless task for a being to have to perform. And yet, that's exactly what they seemed to be doing.

"Kirsten?" Sharman Hix asked. "Any communication you can hear?"

Frieda looked over at Kirsten Simmens sitting inside her pod watching with great concentration through her magnified dome.

"That could be what I heard before," she said. "I'm not sure. And I have to tell you, what I'm seeing makes no sense at all."

"Just what I was thinking," said Frieda.

"Do you see what I see?" Nancy Chow asked the group. "Doesn't that seem like their spit?"

"Yes," three of them answered in unison.

But Kirsten Simmens said, "It's a secretion, but those slits aren't their mouths. I don't think they have mouths. It's more like water pouring through a crack in a rock."

"But they're alive?" Sharman asked.

"They are," Kirsten said. "And the secretions are definitely coming from them, not through them. In other words, it's not coming from the mountain. They're making it."

The team watched in silence for a few minutes. In the time they had been talking, the ice ball had at least doubled in size. But it wasn't rolling down the glassy slope. Something was keeping it stuck to the side of the steep mountain. Maybe something in the wedges' secretions was sticky and held the ball in place.

"Why?" Frieda asked the group in general. "I don't understand the purpose of what they're doing."

"I don't, either," Sharman said. "So let's keep watching."

Another few minutes went by without any change.

But then, a change for sure.

"Look," said Nancy. "Aren't there more of them now?" She pointed toward the mountain.

Frieda strained to see. But Nancy was right. Where there had been six before, now there were more. Maybe ten or twelve.

"Wow," Kirsten said. "Okay, I think I'm getting something."

Frieda looked over at Kirsten sitting in her pod with

her eyes closed. Frieda went back to watching the wedge-shaped creatures, all of them now drooling or secreting or whatever they were doing onto the ball of ice.

It was growing every minute. Now it was a basketball. Still clinging to the edge of the slippery-looking slope, with no sign that it might suddenly start rolling down the mountain.

"Oh," Kirsten mumbled, maybe more to herself than anyone else. "I think ... I think I might understand."

She asked her pod to magnify its dome even more. Frieda followed her lead. Now she could see the creatures as closely as if she were watching them on a computer screen. She could see their facial features, if that was what you'd call them. The triangular-shaped head, the slit across the width, the larger base that was either holding the ice ball in place or maybe holding the creature in place on top of it. That much wasn't clear at all.

Frieda noticed that Kirsten Simmens wasn't watching the ice ball activities anymore. Instead, she was peering into the glassy mountainside itself.

Frieda shifted her focus there, too. She couldn't see anything past the opaque silver-blue ice that made up the mountain. It was like staring into a solid chunk of glass.

But the more she looked, the more she could pick out the contours of the slopes. Just like with the first mountain she had investigated, this one had gentle curves in the long lines, from the tip down to the base. The contours looked like regularly-spaced vertical waves on an otherwise glassy sea.

Kirsten Simmens pointed. "Do you see?"

"See what?" Sharman asked.

Kirsten laughed. "It's an ant hill. Look really, really closely."

Now everyone on the team stared into the glassy center of the mountain. Trying to see what Kirsten saw. So far, Frieda couldn't.

Now Nancy Chow pointed, too. "Yes. I think I see them. Moving down in some kind of ice tunnel, right?"

"Yes," Kirsten said. "Exactly."

Arnie Camper was squinting and staring with all his might. He gave up with a groan. "This reminds me of those magic puzzles I could never see. Someone describe it to me."

Kirsten said, "I can see thousands of them. Tens of thousands—I don't even know. Think of them like a little construction crew in there. Digging out tunnels all through the mountain. Then I think these secretions are what they take out and discard."

"So the big ice balls down on the surface?" Frieda said. "That's what they are? Some kind of construction waste?"

"Must be," Nancy Chow said. "They're trying to move ice out of the tunnels they're digging. So these little creatures are like the waste crew. They carry out the extra ice and spit into these balls."

As if to prove her point, more wedge-shaped creatures appeared lower on the slope and joined the crew already building the ever-increasing ball. It was large enough now—at least two basketballs tall and wide—that it seemed impossible the ball could continue clinging to the slippery glass slope.

But it also explained how there might be hundreds—thousands—of the car-sized ice balls down on the surface of the gray ice that maybe didn't move at all once they hit bottom. Maybe there really was something sticky in the secretions made by the waste crew. Somehow the ball finally broke free from the mountains where the crews were working, but then they stuck wherever they landed.

Everyone on the team was now watching in fascination. Their own personal ant farm, made up of strange ice creatures doing their busy day's work.

But Frieda found her attention drifting. She still felt so uneasy. And she still didn't understand why.

This planet did not seem dangerous. The creatures on that glassy mountain were so foreign and so occupied, they didn't seem to pose any kind of threat to their human visitors.

And since the pods and the pilots inside them were cloaked in material that rendered them invisible to most—although not all, they had learned—beings on either Earth or these other planets, Frieda couldn't understand why her heart had picked up speed and was now beating faster than she wanted.

The ice ball clinging to the side of the silver-blue mountain now looked almost the size of one of the pods. It had grown so much in the last five minutes, Frieda felt disoriented when she looked back at it, having let her attention briefly wander away.

But the sucker looked huge. And the numbers of wedge-shaped creatures had so multiplied, Frieda imagined she might be able to see them from the planet surface, looking up with her naked eyes.

The creatures looked *mean*. It was a strange thought to have. They didn't have eyes with eyebrows angled downward to make them look angry. They didn't have the kinds of mouths—or any mouths at all, according to Kirsten Simmens—that could contort into a snarl. They didn't have hands they could curl into little fists and shake at any intruders. They looked completely benign. No more expressive than a child's building blocks. And yet, looking at them, Frieda felt afraid.

And then. With a crack as loud as thunder—thunder that had just struck right at Frieda's feet—and with the sound amplified by the acoustics of massive glassy mountains all around them and the flat gray ice that stretched out in every direction as far as Frieda could see—

The ball of ice, now larger than any of the pods, suddenly broke free of the mountain slope. Not only broke free, but shot out toward the assembled group like a solid mass of iron exploding from a cannon.

They hadn't taken any precautions. They didn't space themselves defensively at all. The ice ball hit the group square in the center, like a cue ball breaking the cluster of pool balls and sending them shooting toward distant pockets.

Frieda's pod was on the outside, but it took enough of a hit. It went careening backward and to the left, out of control, spinning and rolling, while Frieda tried to slow it or stop it or help it regain its balance in any way.

There were no controls inside the pod. Everything was

done through pilot-to-pod telepathy. But Frieda had nothing to offer her pod. Her mind seemed filled by nothing but swearing.

In its gyroscopic way, Frieda's pod finally rolled back to its proper alignment. Frieda panted with stress. Her heart and lungs were working overtime. Or maybe it was her pod, too, exerting in whatever way it did, adding to Frieda's internal turmoil. Together the two of them felt like a mess.

Frieda gazed out the dome. "Further," she panted. It was still magnified from when she needed to look at the creatures on the mountain. Now she needed to see far away.

The other pods were finding their balance again. The whole team was dispersed.

Arnie Camper was closest, and Frieda could hear him shouting and cursing inside his pod. Then other voices joined with yells and swears of their own.

All of them had been caught off guard. But from what Frieda could see, all of the pods still looked all right.

And the pilots inside them, even though they looked as shaken as Frieda felt, all of them appeared to be upright and whole. So at least that was something.

"Everyone okay?" Sharman called out. "Check in."

"Damn," Arnie Camper said. He blew out a heavy breath. "Yeah, I'm okay. But Shar, what the hell was that?"

"Check in," Sharman said, her voice low and brusk. Sharman's tone always dropped when things were especially serious.

"I'm fine," said Nancy Chow.

"Fine," Frieda said.

"Me, too," said Kirsten Simmens. "I'm sorry, everybody. I … I should have sensed that. I should have…" She trailed off. Frieda looked at her especially pale face. Kirsten looked more shaken than any of them.

"It wasn't your fault," Sharman assured her. "Don't apologize."

"I should have noticed," Kirsten said, still insisting on taking blame. "There was a shift right before. In how they were acting. I just … didn't understand what it was."

"I felt it, too," Frieda said. "But I had no idea what they were going to do. I just thought this whole place was creepy. But how was anybody supposed to know?"

"Gather up," Sharman said. "Over by Frieda. Let's get away from any activity."

The pods began gliding in Frieda's direction. Normally they might cluster up again, but everybody seemed to catch themselves at the same moment. They pulled back, putting space between the pods.

"I think we've seen enough," Sharman said. "Form up."

Even that felt dangerous, but it was the only way to travel back. They needed to be in a line of pods so the transport cylinder could enclose them all like separate cars in a train.

Frieda slipped in behind Arnie Camper. Nancy and Kirsten took positions behind her.

"Arnie, you do it," Sharman said. "What if that thing killed me? You all need to know how to do this."

Sharman talked Arnie through the process. First he asked his pod to encase all the pods together. Then he gave it the coordinates to the Factory, back in the Wasatch Mountain Range outside Salt Lake City, Utah.

"You all need to memorize those coordinates," Sharman said. "You should be able to recite them in your sleep."

Frieda already knew them. For just this reason. It was better to be prepared than to scramble in an emergency. She didn't know how long it would take her to move up in command and have the responsibility of creating the transport, but it didn't hurt to know the details in advance.

"Now you have to think of us," Sharman said. "Think of each of us on the team. You don't want to forget anyone and accidentally leave them behind. So you have us in mind?"

Arnie blew out a breath. Frieda could hear him inside her pod.

"All my ducks in a row," Arnie said. "Sharman, me, Frieda, Nancy, Kirsten. Right? That's all of us?"

He wasn't trying to be funny. Frieda could tell he was being extra careful so his stress wouldn't force a mistake.

"Each of you do it," Sharman said. "Think of us. Like when you created that force field for all of us when we were trapped inside the rock."

Frieda didn't know if it would do any good under their present circumstances, but she wasn't going to object. Whatever Sharman thought could help, Frieda would do.

She still felt shaken, shaken like a pool ball sent careening to the edges of a pool table. Her head still swam a little from the swirling her pod had done. Frieda still felt unsteady.

But she thought of the rest of the team, each of them sitting inside their living pods. She thought of how frightened the pods must have been when that giant ice ball came smashing into their midst. She thought of her fellow explorers, of how much she appreciated their various talents and personalities. She thought of them fondly, and just shifting her mind that way started calming her worried heart.

"Now take us home, Camper," Sharman said. "All of us. Keep us safe. Keep our pods safe."

Camper said, "All together now. Come on, team. Let's go home. I've had it with this place."

He repeated the coordinates for the Factory out loud. Frieda repeated them in her mind. Could she get everyone home safely if it was her turn to act? She thought she could. She felt she was ready.

With a snap of a single motion, the transport cylinder returned them, all in one tight, unified row, back to the beautiful mountains outside the Factory.

Mountains that made sense. That had rocks and trees. That had all sorts of woodland creatures. Some of them might want to hurt her—there were predators out here for sure—but they weren't disguising themselves as little wedge-shaped creatures with nothing more important to do but spit out ice.

Frieda released her pent-up breath. She could hear others on the team doing the same.

"Let's all take a break," Sharman said. "Get some food. Take a shower. Decompress. But I want to meet back in the conference room in two hours and figure out everything that just happened."

It was sound leadership. Frieda appreciated the decision. Everyone was still rattled. It was no good to go into a debrief feeling all keyed up and still confused.

But a shower, some food, some time to let their minds sort out what they saw and heard and felt—that was the right decision. Frieda made a mental note of it. If she were ever in leadership with the team, she hoped she would be smart like Sharman was now.

Once the transport cylinder docked on the concrete floor of the huge hangar hidden inside the mountain, Frieda and the others exited their pods and walked together toward the part of the Factory where their rooms and the cafeterias were.

Frieda walked alongside Kirsten Simmens. Kirsten still looked dejected. Frieda bumped her with her shoulder. "Hey. None of this was your fault. I felt something, too. I just didn't know what it was."

"But I'm supposed to know," Kirsten said. She looked aside at Frieda. "I couldn't hear them. I couldn't understand them. Maybe … maybe the gift is fading."

"Or maybe those little monsters don't speak any kind of language," Frieda said. "Maybe they're just malevolent little a-holes, and they don't say a word before they attack."

Sharman was walking behind them. She obviously heard.

"Save it for the debrief," she told them both. She shook her head. "I'm not sure you're right about it, Frieda. But I agree about Kirsten. You need to get over this. Sometimes a surprise is just a surprise. Get some rest. We'll talk in two."

Frieda always did her best thinking in the shower. There was some kind of magic in turning off her head and letting the water soothe her neck and shoulders. She was hungry, too, but that could wait. She needed to take care of calming herself down first.

The team separated and went their own ways, some to their rooms, some to the nearest cafeteria. Frieda could smell coffee coming from one of the small kitchens where people could prepare their own food. It smelled tempting, but not tempting enough.

Back in her tidy, minimalist room, she peeled off her flight suit. It maintained a certain regular temperature, but Frieda knew she had sweated it up inside.

It would dry out soon enough. She hung it up neatly in her closet. It never seemed to smell, at least not that she could tell, either from her own flight suit or anyone else's. She already knew the material was some kind of modified alien tech. What the world wouldn't pay if they knew there was something that could neutralize the body odors everyone produced all day long.

Her bathroom was clean. She wiped down her sink every morning after she washed her face and brushed her teeth. She did it again at night before she went to bed. It was so much nicer to wake up to clean in the morning. She couldn't understand people who lived like slobs. It would make her nervous and edgy all the time.

The shower stall was glassed in, rather than enclosed with a shower curtain. Frieda undid the band around her curly red hair and let it fall loose around her shoulders.

She turned on the water and stepped into the shower and let her mind begin its gentle work.

Why had she felt so uneasy from the very start? Was it the gray sky, the gray ice that made up the surface, or was it the huge ice balls dotting the ground everywhere she looked? Was it some secret sense that those glass mountains weren't simply strange planetary works of art, but instead were filled with evil little devils who had the power to shoot giant cannon balls toward any intruder?

But the pilots and their pods were supposed to be invisible. That wasn't always true, but maybe it was still mainly true.

And the creatures didn't appear to have eyes or any other way of sensing the pods were there.

But.

Frieda paused in her efforts to comb conditioner through her tangled hair with her fingers.

Why had she felt so uneasy?

The planet. The whole planet. It just felt wrong from the very start.

Frieda finished her shower. She needed to sit and think. The water had done its work, loosening her thoughts. Now she needed to organize what she thought she learned.

She toweled off, combed her unruly hair, and wrapped herself in a thick white terry cloth robe. Then she propped up the pillows on her bed and sat with her back against them and stared at the opposite clean blank wall.

When she was a child, there was one particular grade that gave her trouble for the first time in her life. She loved school. She loved learning. She even loved that teacher. But she absolutely hated going to class.

The elementary school had expanded over time to try to keep up with the growing population. So Frieda's fifth grade class had to meet outside in an auxiliary building, away from the main brick school.

Walking into it made Frieda angry. It was the strangest thing. She started snapping at other kids. She sassed the teacher. She couldn't concentrate. Her test scores took a dive.

By mid-year, she started feeling sick to her stomach every morning. She cried some days, begging her parents to let her stay home. The whole thing was out of hand. She wasn't herself at all.

In desperation, her parents asked the school to let her switch classes. The new teacher was fine, she wasn't any better or worse than the first one, but Frieda thrived. She became her normal happy self. She excelled again. Her test scores shot up. Everything was back on keel.

Why? What was different? The class was held in the main brick school, where Frieda had already spent the previous four grades.

The last week of school, Frieda thought it would be proper and nice to go back to her first teacher and thank her and tell her she was sorry.

The minute, the very second she walked in, the old feelings of anger and depression raced back in.

Frieda could barely wait to get out of there. She waved to the teacher from the door, told her to have a good summer, and turned and escaped as soon as she could.

Years later, Frieda read an article about people who were hypersensitive to certain kinds of lighting.

Retail businesses in particular were starting to refit their lighting to attract more customers.

There was something psychologists called *rage light.* It set people off. It made them grumpy, at best, and actually violent, at worst. Frieda had read that article, and the bell went off in her head.

That auxiliary building in her elementary school must have used that wrong kind of lighting.

And the gray-skied planet, Ice Planet 2—did it have something similar about it that made Frieda feel it?

It wasn't just the sky. It was also the balls of ice on the ground and the silver-blue glassy mountains that dominated the charcoal sky. Maybe all of them together created a similar effect. And maybe Frieda was the only one on the team who had that strange hypersensitivity that made her want to leave it as soon as they got there.

But what did that mean, in terms of their survival? Was it some kind of warning Frieda could learn how to heed?

Her fifth grade classroom hadn't felt dangerous. The teacher was perfectly nice. If this was some kind of evolutionary adaptation, it didn't seem to serve Frieda in any useful way.

Unless it was for some future application, and that future was finally now.

Maybe people who were sensitive to the subtlest of environmental conditions had some vital work to do—just not right away. The people who couldn't stand loud music. The ones who felt drained being around people in general.

The sensitives who couldn't bear certain kinds of smells—what if there was a reason, and it just had to be discovered?

Could Frieda's anger and edginess on Ice Planet 2 have been a tool she could learn how to wield? She had already learned how to connect to her pod telepathically. Was there another level of communication she could learn, amplifying her feelings into some kind of useful intel?

The idea was so exciting, she jumped up from her bed and quickly got dressed. The meeting was still at least an hour away, but she could be ready. She could organize her ideas.

Frieda dressed in soft pants and an equally soft shirt. Her skin was sensitive to the harshness of stiff cotton and certain synthetics.

She had felt so high maintenance about her clothes for so much of her life. But it wasn't worth putting up with things that hurt or itched or just felt wrong against her sensitive skin, just to try to be less of a pain in the rear.

She braided her wet hair. She always had to use special shampoo and conditioner to keep it tamed. And she had special soaps and special lotions. Nothing was just standard, like everybody else used.

But Frieda was beginning to see it all through a different lens now.

Maybe she had been made this way for a reason.

Wasn't it possible that people were being born right now who had certain difficulties and peculiarities that might not make sense right now, but that would make them perfect for some situation in the future?

The non-verbal children who saw patterns that no one

else could see. The obsessives who spent hours every day learning the minutia about whatever it was that captured their attention. All of the so-called freaks of whatever particular variety—what if they were just waiting in reserve until the human race needed exactly what they were and what they had to offer?

Frieda slipped on her softest socks and her favorite pair of comfortable shoes. She tidied up her room before she left it.

Then she took her particular sensitivities and her private peculiarities with her down to the cafeteria for hot tea with the exact amount of honey and lemon and to find some food that would perfectly hit the spot.

She was who she was. Just like Kirsten Simmens was who she was, able to hear alien languages if they bothered to speak.

But Frieda Wiles could understand the language of sky and mountain and ice. The language of color and light and shape.

And next time she would know: Danger, get out. It was just a feeling—and that feeling was a gift she had been born with.

It was time to pay attention. Her feelings were *right*.

THE GRASSLANDS OF
PLANET ONYX GREEN

1

Julie Trident wandered the halls of the Factory, looking for anything better to do. She had been on medical leave for five weeks now, and even though she still wasn't one hundred percent, she was at least ninety. Eighty-five.

She had already worked out for an hour in the second-floor gym, concentrating on leg lifts and squats and lunges. Having strong legs made her whole body feel stronger.

She still wore her workout pants, sneakers, and a sweaty T-shirt, but she didn't feel like going back to her room just yet to shower and change. She needed company. She needed conversation. This enforced convalescence was driving her crazy.

Julie was thirty-seven, slim and fit, with dark eyes, tan skin, and thick brown hair she wore to her shoulders and usually kept in a low ponytail. Right now her hair was loose for no other reason than that she wanted some variety. She was that desperate. She might even cut it shorter herself today just out of boredom.

Julie peered into the second-floor cafeteria to see if anyone she knew was in there. But it was mid-morning, too late for breakfast and too early for lunch, and everyone else had work to do.

Julie went inside the cafeteria anyway. Ronda, one of the cooks, was back behind the food service line concocting something that involved a whole lot of grated cheese.

"I want that," Julie called out to her as she grabbed two coffee to-go cups and filled them at self-serve counter.

"I know you do," Ronda said. She held up her gloved hands to show Julie they were coated with cheese, something that might be cream, and what looked like bread crumbs. Ronda was younger than Julie by at least a decade, and looked like she should be on television, not hidden in a kitchen inside the Factory's underground warren, serving scientists and pilots and designers and whoever else was staying at the Factory at the moment.

"Lunch or dinner?" Julie asked, snapping the lids on her to-go cups.

"Dinner. So go take a nap or something."

Julie gave her a friendly smile. Ronda was obviously just joking around. But the comment bit. Obviously everyone knew that Julie was spending her days just lazing around. Julie left the cafeteria with two cups full of steaming coffee and a mood much darker than the one she went in with.

She was used to doing things. All the time. As a little

girl, if she wasn't on her bike, riding around with the kids in the neighborhood, she was swimming or running or playing soccer or softball or basketball and otherwise staying out of her mother's hair.

Julie's father died when she was just a baby. Her mother, Dr. Caroline Baird, a biologist, like Julie, mostly raised her alone. There were grandparents who pitched in often enough, but otherwise it was just Julie and her mother.

Julie made the turn at the end of the corridor beyond the cafeteria and continued walking down the spur to the left. There were no placards on any of the doors announcing what the rooms were or who was inside them. You either knew or you didn't. Julie knew.

She cradled both coffees in her left arm and placed her right hand against the lighted blue square in the center of the door. The pad recognized her handprint and Julie could hear the lock click. She turned the handle and carried the coffees inside.

She could see her mother sitting at her desk at the back of the room, typing on her computer. The computer screen was on an articulating arm that allowed Julie's mother to pull it as close to her face as she could. The lettering on the screen was so large, Julie could read it from the back of the room.

Caroline had written, *Piece 55. Green dust. Former rock?*

"Hi, Mom," Julie said. Her mother jumped. She must not have heard the door open.

If her hearing was going now too…

Julie hated to see her mother's deterioration.

But Caroline Baird's mind still seemed as sharp as ever. It was just her eyesight and maybe her hearing that were going.

And she always looked so tired to Julie. Like she might sleep only a few hours a night.

"Sweetheart," Caroline said, swiveling her chair around and standing ready with a hug.

Julie set down the coffees on her mother's desk and gathered her gray-haired mother in her arms.

"What are you working on?" Julie asked. She handed her mother one of the coffees.

"Oh, thanks," Caroline said. She swept her hand over the papers on her desk. "Just more cataloging. There's always more to do."

Julie nodded. But she wasn't convinced. Her mother had been cataloging Julie's grandfather's artifacts for decades now. How could there be any more to do there? But Julie didn't question it. She respected her mother's ways, even if they didn't always make sense.

And the truth was, Dr. Caroline Baird had made so many contributions to the designs and manufacturing of experimental aircraft and equipment and technical clothing used at the Factory, who was Julie to say her mother's methods didn't work?

"What are you up to today?" Caroline asked her.

Julie shrugged. "Nothing. At all. Going crazy just sitting around."

"Just another week," Caroline said.

Julie nodded. She took a sip of the bitter black coffee. Dr. Tognocci, the Factory's in-house physician, had told

Julie she had to rest and recuperate for six full weeks. Now that Julie was feeling so much stronger, she would love to get back to doing expeditions with Sharman Hix and the rest of the team, but Dr. Tognocci was a Rottweiler about it and wouldn't set Julie free.

Julie had tried sneaking out for the team's latest expedition, but the team leader, Sharman Hix, wouldn't allow it.

"Tognocci will put my head in a vice," Sharman said. She rested her hand on Julie's arm and gave her a sympathetic look. "Just another week," she said before taking off this morning.

That was all anyone could say. *Another week, another week.*

That, or *Go take a nap.* Julie had to shake off that obviously joking remark.

Here in her mother's lab, Julie always liked to wander and look around. It wasn't like an ordinary biology lab. Julie had spent plenty of years in those.

Caroline Baird had inherited a trove of artifacts from her father, Dr. Travis Baird. He was a UFO investigator in the 1960s and 70s. Later he became a best-selling science fiction writer.

Julie had chosen her last name from the name of his most popular character, Dr. Max Trident, biologist, adventurer, and a UFO and alien investigator.

Julie knew from her mother that many of the experiences Dr. Max Trident had with alien beings were not, in fact, fiction. They were Julie's grandfather's thinly-veiled attempt to bring the truth to the general public.

Julie gestured with her cup toward the writing on her mother's computer screen. "What green dust?"

"Oh." Caroline Baird chuckled lightly, as if she might be slightly embarrassed. But Julie knew her mother too well. It really meant she was about to tell a fib.

"It's nothing," Caroline said. "Just something I thought about in the middle of the night. The label on one of your grandfather's old boxes said *Cortez 1964 rock*. But all that was in there was a little pile of green dust. So I was just wondering last night what kind of rock that might have been. I already ran tests on it a long time ago, but ... maybe with the current equipment I could look at it again."

"Is it an alien rock?" Julie asked, already knowing the answer was yes.

"It might be," her mother said. She shrugged. "Just something I want to put out of my mind."

Julie knew there was more to the story, but she decided not to press. Her mother had reams of notebooks from Travis Baird and a storehouse full of his artifacts. She seemed to spend as much time revisiting his old research as pursuing her own. Caroline never seemed to live entirely in the present.

Whereas Julie was feeling every single minute of the present slowly plodding by. She needed some more exercise. Maybe she would climb the metal stairs out to the top of the facility and spend a few hours roaming around in the woods. The Factory was embedded in the side of a mountain in the Wasatch Mountain Range near Salt Lake City, Utah. It was late August and Julie had already noticed some of the aspen leaves starting to turn. A fresh breeze and some exploring would do her restless body and mind some good.

"I'll let you get back to work," she told her mother.

"I'm so glad when you stop by," Caroline said, but Julie noticed her mother didn't try to make her stay. She was preoccupied with something. Julie knew the feeling.

She kissed her mother on the cheek. "Get some sleep, Mom. You know I worry about you."

"Who can sleep?" Caroline asked. "Too many mysteries of the universe to solve." She smiled as she said it, but Julie knew her mother was serious.

At times, Julie felt the same way.

And it was why she was itching to get back to active duty.

Sharman Hix and the exploratory team were out there visiting another planet right now. Discovering new organisms, new terrain, who knew what else.

If only Julie had followed Sharman's order not to try to help a creature who was stuck on a planet's moon, Julie wouldn't have had to go on medical leave for six full weeks. Her body had paid a high price.

But now the enforced inactivity was too much punishment on top of that. Julie had learned her lesson.

She left her mother sitting with her face practically touching her computer screen. Julie only wished Dr. Tognocci could do something to help Caroline Baird's vision.

But it was a condition Dr. Tognocci couldn't correct or cure. Julie suspected the reason why, but she wouldn't expose her mother's secret.

Julie was just making the turn to go back to her room to change into warmer clothes to go outside when a young woman came whipping around the corner. Julie recognized her from the underground hangar where all the experimental aircraft were kept. She thought the woman might be on the maintenance team. She wasn't sure. The name on her green work shirt said Viv.

Viv skidded to a halt barely in time to keep from running into Julie. "Oh, good," she said breathlessly. She must have run all the way from the hangar. "I'm supposed to find you. Message from Sharman Hix."

Julie didn't like the sound of that. Sharman was supposed to be out with the team for the entire day. They were mapping a planet they had already visited a few times over the past two weeks. Julie should have been with them, riding around in her sphere-shaped pod above the planet like the rest of them, observing and mapping what they saw.

"She says be ready," Viv said. "She's coming back for you in ten minutes."

There had to be something wrong for Sharman to ignore Julie's enforced medical leave, but at the moment, Julie didn't care what the reason was.

She gave Viv a smile and took off at a run toward her room.

Finally. *Finally.*

Julie Trident was back in action.

2

Julie wasn't sure what to expect. She didn't know if Sharman was coming back alone or with the rest of the team.

It was just Sharman.

The petite African American pilot was waiting outside her individual pod. She wore her matte gray flight suit with the hood pulled up over the back of her head, and she didn't look relaxed at all. She stood barefoot on the cold concrete floor of the hangar. Julie knew Sharman preferred to pilot her pod skin to skin with her feet and hands touching the interior of her craft, but usually she put on her soft black boots again as soon as she landed somewhere.

Not this time. She was obviously in a hurry.

Julie didn't need to be told that. As soon as she saw Sharman she jogged across the hangar to where Sharman's pod sat at the front of a line of fifty others.

Julie looked around for her own pod. Even though technically she had trained to fly any of them, she had grown attached to her own pod. It had pitched in on the moon of Oasis to help rescue her, and Julie wanted to stick with it if she could.

"Get in," Sharman said.

Julie glanced skeptically at Sharman's pod.

"It'll fill out. Just climb in after me." Sharman stepped over the lip of the open sphere. Its clear dome top was tucked neatly inside the rim.

Julie positioned herself behind Sharman's pilot's seat and lifted her leg up and over. Sharman was right. As soon as the pod felt Julie's boot touch its interior, it began reshaping itself, elongating, making room for Julie to sit on the floor behind Sharman's seat.

"I'm still training this one," Sharman said. "It doesn't know it can make a second seat yet. But it shouldn't be too bad. Short ride."

Julie settled onto the floor. Sharman was right, it wasn't that uncomfortable. The metal inside the sphere had a little give to it, making it feel slightly padded. As soon as Julie figured out which way she wanted to sit, leaning against one interior wall and drawing her knees up in front of her, the pod seemed to reshape its floor to Julie's contours. Maybe it was just her imagination, but she wouldn't be all that surprised. The pods were living organisms, not just cold metal machines. As the clear dome lid came up and over them both, Julie could see the pod had changed the shape of that too into an oval rather than round. They were good to go.

"I got you some gear," Sharman said, pointing to a small pack like the one all the pilots on her team kept stowed inside the footwells of their pods. "I don't plan on getting out," Sharman added, "but just in case."

Julie didn't need to check the pack. She knew that inside would be a few emergency rations like energy bars and water, along with the strange head gear her mother had had a hand in developing. It grew around a person's head and supplied the necessary oxygen and other gases they needed to breathe.

But the pods did that too. As long as she and Sharman stayed inside, it wouldn't matter what the planet's atmosphere had to offer. And even though Julie wasn't nearly as comfortable as she might have been sitting in her own pilot's chair in her own pod instead of scrunched up on the floor, she wasn't going to argue about staying inside. She was just glad to be going out on the expedition at all.

Sharman piloted her pod straight up to the ceiling of the hangar. There were small openings there that allowed the pods to squeeze out like bubbles escaping from a bottle.

Once they were outside Julie took a moment to admire the beauty of the landscape. There were more yellowing aspens that even just a few days ago when she had last been outside. But she could walk in the woods any time. Right now she was more interested in traveling somewhere into space.

Sharman didn't speak to her pod out loud. She was too advanced for that. But Julie knew that Sharman must have given the pod the coordinates of where to travel, because the next thing Julie knew the mountains near the Factory disappeared, replaced by a deep velvety blackness that felt like being inside a cocoon.

"That's Onyx Green," Sharman said, pointing to a planet down beneath them.

"Oh my god, it's gorgeous," Julie said. She could understand why Sharman or someone else on the team had named it that.

The planet reminded her of Jupiter with its horizontal stripes of brown and peach and light blue. But this planet had alternating bands of black and a dark, rich green.

"I wanted you to see it first," Sharman said. "We're going to one of the green sectors."

"Where's everyone else?" Julie asked.

"Down there waiting. Watching. You'll see."

Sharman must have given her pod new coordinates, because in a blink the darkness of space disappeared, replaced by scenery Julie didn't expect to see anywhere but on Earth.

She shifted forward onto her knees to get a better look out of the pod's dome.

"Oh," Julie said.

"I know. Kind of creepy, isn't it?"

"Uh … yeah. In a way."

The other four members of the team welcomed Julie through the pod comms. All they had to do was speak inside their own crafts, and Julie could hear them as easily as if they were sitting next to her.

She gave them all a general, half-hearted wave. She was too distracted by the landscape below.

It was as if someone had been told to make a model of a forest out of trees that were totally mismatched. There were the equivalent of giant redwoods growing next to short, spindly juniper bushes, next to tall evergreens sandwiched between twisted, gnarled trees that might be oaks if they grew on Earth.

And that was just the forest.

Encircling the hodgepodge of trees was a wide band of grasslands where the grass might be ten feet tall. Julie couldn't tell from here. Her perspective felt completely off.

The grasslands might be five or ten miles wide. Then beyond them was another forest full of more mismatched trees.

Whoever put this landscape together had a bizarre sense of design.

"Okay," Sharman said. "We just started looking at this section today. So all of this is still new to us."

"The rest of the planet isn't like this?" Julie asked.

"Not at all. It's full of weird plants we've never seen, but at least it looks normal. But it's not just the trees in this section," Sharman said. "It's the animals."

Julie hadn't noticed a single animal before, but now, just because Sharman said that, her eyes adjusted to a different view. Or maybe Sharman's pod did that for her. The clear domes sometimes acted on their own as magnifiers. Julie wasn't sure at the moment which it was.

But looking down at the tall grasslands that were waving

in whatever the planet had for wind, she could see dark shapes just barely visible above the grass. They were moving slowly. Whatever the animals were, they appeared to be grazing.

As Julie's eyes began to pick them out among the grass, she realized there must be a hundred or more of the animals in that field. Maybe two hundred. She could see the tops of their heads, black dots against the green, raising and lowering as the creatures ate their way through the grass.

"What are they?" Julie asked.

"I saw a few of them up close," Sharman said. "The best I can call them is dog-sheep. They look like huge dogs with thick black coats you could make a blanket out of."

Julie strained to try to see better. So far all she could see was the tops of their heads. But she saw a few pairs of ears that did look generally canine.

"How big are they?" she asked. "I can't tell."

"Oh, I'd say bison."

"Wow." Julie stared down at the grazing herd. Now that Sharman had given her that perspective, she saw the whole scene with sharper focus. She didn't know specifically, but she guessed that a bison might stand about six feet tall. Which meant the grass was about that height too. Those bison had some good feeding on Onyx Green's prairie.

Unlike bison, they did not appear to have horns. If Sharman was right, and they all had dog faces poking out of their thick, shaggy coats, then what a strange and yet potentially adorable new species this might be.

"But that's not the most interesting part," Sharman said. "I brought you here for something else."

Julie looked around. "What?"

"You have to wait for it. But it shouldn't take long. We saw it twice in about an hour."

Julie took a moment to reposition herself inside the pod. She was still kneeling, peering out the window, and was grateful for the cushioned floor against her knees.

But she couldn't really see as well as she wanted.

"Can we go lower?"

"It's better from up here," Sharman said. "So you can get the whole situation at a glance."

Julie was about to ask her more about it when Kirsten Simmens's voice came into the pod. "They're coming." Julie looked at Kirsten, floating about five feet away in her own pod. She was in her forties, with short ash-blonde hair, a nice woman with a unique ability to hear and understand foreign languages. That included the languages of at least some extraterrestrials.

Julie looked to where Kirsten was pointing. Everyone turned in the same direction to watch. Julie saw movement among the odd, mismatched trees. Something scurrying down the huge trunk of what looked as enormous as a redwood. Not just a few things scurrying down it, a *lot*.

Then Sharman pointed to their right. Back where the forest seemed made up of triangular-shaped trees with dark green branches that made them look like pine trees.

Julie thought she saw a flash of dark orange. Some creature running between the trees.

Then she saw more of them. And she knew.

Bile shot up through her throat.

"No," she said. "*No.*"

"Just watch," Sharman said. Her voice was completely unsympathetic, even though Julie had told her enough of the stories.

It couldn't be. It couldn't. Julie watched in horror, afraid to see that it was true.

Running through the pine trees, then past the gnarled oaks, past the other mismatched trees large and small, was a pack of the worst aliens Julie had ever faced in her previous occupation.

What her colleagues called LPs. Lizard People. A humorous-sounding name for something that killed with such ferocity and speed, Julie had hoped never ever to see one alive again.

But this was obviously their home planet. Or maybe they had infiltrated many planets—how could she know? She stared down at the racing bodies and felt a sick twisting inside her gut.

The adults were seven feet tall. Dark brown or burnt-orange rough skin. Heads shaped like iguanas, with a rounded skull tapering down to a narrow snout. Rows of sharp, ripping teeth along both sides of their mouths. Like sharks on two legs, but with reptilian eyes that had vertical pupils.

And the way they smelled. A sickening, musky odor that turned out to affect humans' nervous systems, making them freeze up, get dreamy and lethargic, not realize the risk and just stay where they were to get devoured.

The LPs especially enjoyed ripping off legs and arms, then cracking them open and sucking out the meat inside, like someone breaking open a lobster leg and savoring the tender meat.

Julie had watched the LPs kill people she knew. She had fled for her life from a pack of them, certain any second they would catch up to her with their long, muscular legs and tackle her and start ripping and rending—

Julie's face broke out in a sweat. She had to swallow hard to keep from getting sick.

Sharman glanced at her and must have seen the look on Julie's face.

"I know," Sharman said. "I'm sorry. But I need you to see this. It's not going to be what you think."

Julie tightened her lips. She gave Sharman a sharp nod. Dammit, this wasn't what she wanted to come back to. It would be better to be napping back in her room at the Factory, or wandering the halls bored out of her mind.

Sharman pointed to the edge of the grassy plain. "Now watch."

The swarm of movement Julie had seen coming down the huge redwood had now reached the forest floor. The swarm continued onward toward the grassland. Like a huge mass of light brown, so close together Julie couldn't begin to count how many there were.

And the LPs were right behind them. Shooting forward from the cover of trees to try to catch any stragglers at the back of the mass.

"Closer," Julie said, not even realizing she said it. Sharman's pod obeyed her desire. It magnified the view through the dome. Now Julie could see the individual creatures.

They were a buff color, halfway between yellow and brown. Judging from the height of the grass and the dog-sheep nearby, each creature might be only a foot or two tall. There must be a thousand down there, all pressing forward in panic toward the grazing dog-sheep. Then the mass broke up, the creatures went in separate forward directions, all of them seeking the closest dog-sheep to jump onto and cling to their thick shaggy coats.

Once they came to rest on the dog-sheep, Julie could see the details of the creatures more clearly. They looked like a cross between monkeys and tree frogs. They had big round eyes in their round faces, squat plump bodies, a pair of monkey-like arms in front and longer frog legs in back, each appendage ending in four fingers or toes with bulbous, rounded tips.

And Julie could see the dog-sheep more closely now too. They were, as she imagined they might be, adorable. They had huge heads like furry Tibetan Mastiffs, with long black jowls and manes of such thick black fur they almost looked like lions.

While the fur around their faces looked straight, on their bodies it lay in heaps of curls and coils. Julie had been to a sheep farm once, and the farmer encouraged her to bury her hands in one of the sheep's coats.

"It's lanolin," the farmer said. "Can you feel it?"

Julie could. She pulled her hands out and rubbed her fingers together. They felt soft, as though they'd just been bathed in lotion.

Julie could imagine sticking her hands into the thick

coats of these dog-sheep and seeing her arms disappear halfway to her elbows, the coats looked that deep.

And the animals were grazers like sheep. The name dog-sheep seemed to fit. But they weren't just passive grazers out in the field.

As soon as the little ones, the monkey-frogs, latched onto them, sometimes ten or twenty to an animal, the dog-sheep raised their heads, alert to the coming danger. Julie could see the dog-sheep pulling back their mouths into snarls.

But the LPs kept coming. They raced into the grass and scooped up as many of the loose monkey-frogs they could find. And much to Julie's dismay, they tore off the little creatures' arms and legs and popped them into their hungry mouths before following up with the plump little bodies. Why go to the trouble of breaking them apart, rather than eating them whole? Each little monkey-frog could have fit in an LP's mouth in one gulp.

But the LPs must like it that way. Nature didn't make mistakes. It was an adaptation that had evolved for some reason.

And it was how the LPs were on Earth too. They started with the legs, then ripped off the arms, and only then got to the human bodies.

Julie had a flash of memory of what she saw during at attack in Wyoming. She gave her head a sharp shake to make the image go away.

The LPs were still pushing into the grassland, but by now the herd of dog-sheep had turned the other way. They had a slow, loping run that looked too slow from Julie's vantage. The LPs were lightning fast. It was one of the most terrifying things about them. But the dog-sheep must be running faster than Julie could judge, because the herd had a good head start on the pursuing predators.

Then one of the LPs pressing closest to the front managed to swipe a little monkey-frog from the back of the dog-sheep it had attached itself to.

The dog-sheep must have felt it, or maybe the little creature cried out as the LP grabbed it, because the dog-sheep whirled around with an agility Julie didn't expect and it launched into an attack.

The dog-sheep's maw opened wide and clamped onto the LP's arm. Then it shook the LP so hard, Julie could see the LP's feet spring off of the ground.

The dog-sheep never released its grip. It kept shaking the LP every which way, and Julie watched in satisfaction as the LP's head snapped right and then left, and then lolled back on its broken spine.

"Did you see that?" Sharman asked.

"Yeah."

"That's what happens. Keep watching. I think you'll like it."

Sharman flashed her a grin. Julie ventured a smile of her own. Sharman hadn't brought her out here to torture her with horrible memories, but to offer her some relief from everything she had witnessed.

"More coming," Kirsten said.

Julie looked to her right. There was another wave of LPs breaking from the trees.

It seemed like a lot of risk for very little meat. The monkey-frogs were barely a morsel.

But now Julie saw the strategy. There was a first wave and a second. The second wave was going for bigger game.

But the dog-sheep weren't stupid. The ones closest to the LPs now turned to fight.

Four or five LPs tried to circle one dog-sheep and isolate it from the others.

Julie had watched wolves in the wild. She had observed their pack behavior when they hunted. There was an elegance to it, even though she hated seeing the deer and elk lose almost every time.

The LPs weren't elegant. They were clumsy and over confident. Two or three would rush in at once, trying to overwhelm the dog-sheep, but the bison-sized animal was a ferocious opponent.

And not only that, the other dog-sheep didn't simply stand by. They rushed in and overwhelmed the LPs instead.

Julie watched one LP after another get the same treatment she had watched before. Jaws clamping tightly on an arm or a leg or a neck, then the violent shaking until the spine or neck snapped.

The dog-sheep didn't seem interested in the LPs' flesh. They truly were herbivores. Once the attacker was dead, the dog-sheep spat out whatever part they held in their mouths.

It was fascinating to watch. Julie had never seen a species like it.

And all during the attacks, the little monkey-frogs still

hung on. There must be something in the bulbous tips of their fingers that gave them extra grip in the thick curly fur. Or maybe, just like Julie at the sheep farm, they stuck their fingers in deep to where maybe the dog-sheep's coat was sticky inside instead of soft like lanolin.

This was a biologist's dream. Julie could spend the next year of her life studying these grassland and forest creatures.

But not the LPs. She never wanted to see one again. Even if it was in the process of being shaken to death by a massive dog-sheep.

And then, just as quickly as it began, the attack was over and the LPs raced out of the grass.

The closest dog-sheep loped after them, their lips still pulled back in their intimidating snarls. The little buff-colored creatures clung to them like barnacles on the side of a ship.

"So what was the point of that?" Julie asked. It was more a question for herself than for Sharman, but Sharman answered.

"I guess if they actually took down one of those dog-sheep every now and then, they'd be able to eat for at least a few days."

"Yeah, but it's too inefficient," Julie said. Her specialty had been predators who lived above 8,000 feet in the western mountains of the US. She had watched more hunts than she cared to remember.

"You're not going to believe this," Kirsten Simmens broke in, "but I don't think they're doing it for the food. I think they're doing it because it's fun."

Julie tilted her head and gave Kirsten a deadpan look from across their two pods. "Come on. That isn't the reason."

Kirsten shrugged. "It's just a feeling. They don't have any kind of language I understand, but there's just something about the way they're acting. I don't know. Just a theory."

Sharman chuckled. "Anyone else want to chime in? Julie's only seen it once, but you've all seen it three times now. What does anyone think?"

While the team offered a few theories of their own, Julie gazed down at the grasslands below.

The dog-sheep had gone back to peacefully grazing. The monkey-frogs had mostly let go of all their protectors and were gathering together at the edge of the grassy plain.

The dome on Sharman's pod was still magnifying the view. Julie started counting as many of the little creatures as she could see.

She got to the point where she could estimate them based on the size of the various clusters. She started estimating them by twenties, counting all the way up to eight hundred.

Eight hundred. That was a lot of tasty treats. Was it worth the LPs fighting against the dog-sheep to get them?

Or was it, like Kirsten Simmens suggested, just a fun exercise in chasing them and making them run? Occasionally they might catch a few and snap them apart and pop them into their mouths.

Predators didn't risk their lives for sport.

At least not very often.

Now that she thought of it, Julie remembered reading a scientific paper in college by someone who had been following polar bears across Alaska.

Even though the polar bears hunted seals and needed a lot of them to keep up their weight, the researcher had seen something he couldn't explain in any other way: he saw the polar bears playing.

One of them had set aside the head of a seal he had just eaten. And instead of finishing off the meal, he batted the head to another bear.

The two of them rolled it back and forth across the ice like it was a soccer ball or a hockey puck.

Neither of them ever ruined the game by giving in and eating the head. The researcher watched in amazement as even more bears joined in.

Finally, whether because they were tired of the game or just hungry, one of the bears chomped down on the head and then others came to join it.

So was it possible that was what the LPs were doing here? Bored, the way Julie had been bored earlier in the day, and deciding to go work out for a while by chasing monkey-frogs and tussling it up with the dog-sheep?

This was a different planet than Earth. Obviously its species could live by completely different rules.

But although Julie was curious, as any scientist would be, she knew in her heart she would have to let this one go.

She already knew more than she wanted about the LPs who had somehow made it to Earth. That, in itself, was a question for a curious scientist to pursue. How did the LPs get from one planet to another? They were obviously too primitive a species to design and make their own ships.

Another scientist would want to study the dog-sheep and the monkey-frogs and whatever other fascinating animals might exist on this planet.

A botanist would want to study that strange collection of trees. It made no sense for them to grow together like that, but the organisms on this planet obviously lived by different rules.

It was the reason for exploration like Sharman Hix and her team were doing.

It was a worthy use of time and energy and effort to gain knowledge of a planet so unique.

But Dr. Julie Trident was not the scientist for the job. She would rather remain ignorant of the mysteries of Onyx Green than have to put herself through a nightmare again.

Maybe someone else would be ashamed to walk away like this, but Julie wasn't ashamed. She only felt mildly tired.

"Thank you for showing me," she told Sharman.

"Was I right to?" Sharman asked.

Julie gave her a sad smile. "The truth? I'm not really sure."

There had been so much grief in her past. So much heartache when she learned the truth. She realized how little she knew about how world really worked. She learned that the people she thought were in charge weren't the true powers at all. And Julie and everyone like her was just a pawn. Just tools to be used.

But working with the people at the Factory, working with her mother and the other scientists and engineers and pilots and everyone else, had given Julie back some of the faith she had lost.

She didn't have to prove herself to anyone anymore. And she didn't have to take every mission. She wasn't a Marine anymore, she didn't work for the government, she was a free agent, free to follow where her curiosity and her heart led her.

"I should probably take you back," Sharman said. "Before anyone knows I sneaked you out."

Julie turned away from the view and sat back down on the floor of the pod.

Sharman was watching her, maybe worried Julie wasn't feeling very well. It was true, Julie wasn't as strong as she was five weeks ago, but she could feel herself coming back.

"Maybe someday," she told Sharman, in response to an unspoken question.

Sharman nodded, as if the answer satisfied her.

"That's enough for today," Sharman told the team. Julie watched the others fly their pods into line behind Sharman's. Then Sharman activated the clear transport cylinder to encase all them in a row.

Julie closed her eyes and leaned back against the wall of the pod while Sharman communicated the coordinates to take them back home.

Maybe someday. Maybe. Julie didn't have to decide definitively right now. Maybe in time she would want to come back out to Planet Onyx Green and explore it with everyone else.

Study the sweet-looking little creatures who clung to the dog-faced bison grazing in the grass. Maybe that was where her future would take her.

Or maybe Julie could decide that even though another scientist could shake off her past and just coldly do her work, Julie wasn't that scientist.

She had a tender heart. Maybe it wasn't ideal for the various paths she had taken so far, but it felt pretty ideal for the person she wanted to be now.

When she opened her eyes again the afternoon sun streamed down through the late summer aspens on the hillside beside the Factory, showing off the ones that didn't want to wait until autumn to turn gold.

Julie reached forward and gave Sharman's hand a squeeze. "Thank you. You made the right call."

Sharman turned her head to the side and met Julie's gaze. "Okay. Good. I wasn't sure."

"But maybe leave me off the roster for that one," Julie said. "At least for a while."

"You're out on medical leave," Sharman snapped, all business again. "I don't know what you're talking about. I'm not taking you anywhere."

Julie had forgotten that everyone else in their pods could hear their discussion too, until Sharman said a little more loudly, "Correct?"

"We sure miss her," someone else on the team chimed in. And then the others had their witty little remarks to add.

The transport cylinder angled downward toward the

Factory with Sharman's pod in the lead. Julie was sorry to go back inside again.

The sky above Onyx Green had been even bluer than the one here. It was a beautiful place. Strange and beautiful, populated by plants and animals that were still gnawing at Julie's curiosity.

Maybe she would go back after all. Maybe she could watch the LPs from a distance and some day not break out in a sick, cold sweat.

Maybe she was assuming she was more damaged than she actually was.

Maybe she was regaining her strength in more ways than one.

Julie bid her teammates goodbye and left them to sort through their gear and to put away their pods. For once, Julie had no post-expedition obligations.

She could go dress warmly, like she planned earlier in the day, and go topside to take a walk through the woods.

But she was hungry now, and if she had to admit it, she was tired.

And after the stress of the expedition, she needed something else.

Someone else. Sometimes a girl just needed her mother.

And Julie had the feeling her mother needed her too. Maybe it was to start paying her old mother more attention.

Ronda in the cafeteria had promised something cheesy and bready for dinner tonight. And there was usually ice cream for anyone who wanted it.

As Julie made her way through the warren of corridors to her mother's lab, she had a flash of the little buff-colored creatures clinging to their big shaggy protectors grazing in the grasses.

There was nothing wrong with seeking a little help now and then.

Nothing wrong with hiding if you thought you were in trouble.

But you use that sanctuary to lick your wounds and get better. You shake yourself off. You figure out a way to get back into action again.

She had been resting enough. Hiding enough. Trying to block out the pain of her memories for too long.

Julie had wanted to be a scientist all of her life. And here she was. There were new discoveries out there for the taking. Julie just had to go, and see, and learn.

As she walked through the corridors, Julie could feel strength in her steps again. The outing had done her good. In more ways than one.

She would go back to Onyx Green the next time Sharman invited her. And this time she would let go of the fear that had been strangling her tender heart.

Julie placed her hand against the lighted square in the center of her mother's door. She could hear the lock click open. Julie poked her head in and invited her mother to dinner.

Tonight they would talk mother to daughter, biologist to biologist, explorer to explorer.

There was still so much to know, a whole universe full

of fascinating and wonderful worlds, and the only way to learn was to keep investigating with an open and curious mind.

Julie's long convalescence was over. It was time to climb back on the path of science.

More in the Dove Season Universe
MAKER

- A mechanical genius joins a top-secret mission to learn about alien technology from the aliens themselves. What he discovers changes everything.
- A linguist with the unique ability to communicate with anyone—human or otherwise—uncovers the secrets of an alien race.
- At an elite science conference at a remote mountain retreat, a theoretical physicist learns that her theories are closer to reality than she thought. But even her wildest imaginings do not prepare her for the truth.
- What if death is only one possible outcome, and there are ways to continue a life? For a grieving husband, the only choice is to find his wife again.

A standalone collection in the Dove Season Universe. The future is what we make it.

ABOUT THE AUTHOR

Robin Brande is an award-winning author, former trial attorney, black belt in martial arts, Reiki Master, and wilderness medic. Her outdoor adventures range from the Rocky Mountains to the Alps to Iceland.

She writes in multiple genres, including mystery, adventure, fantasy, science fiction, young adult, romance, and self-help.

For more information:
https://robinbrande.com/

For updates about upcoming installments of DOVE SEASON, along with previews and special discounts, subscribe to the Robin Brande newsletter: https:// robinbrande.com/pages/subscribe.

MORE FROM ROBIN BRANDE

SHOW YOUR BOOK-LOVING STYLE!

AND SCIENCE LOVING, ART LOVING, DOG AND CAT LOVING, AND MORE...

Treat yourself to a soft, comfy, custom-made T-shirt designed by Robin Brande herself, inspired by her own books. You can see all of them at robinbrande.com/collections/t-shirts.

And here's a secret just for you: Use the discount code **READER10** at checkout to get **10% off any items in the store**. That means books, T-shirts, hoodies, mugs—whatever you'd like. Go ahead and treat yourself, book lover.

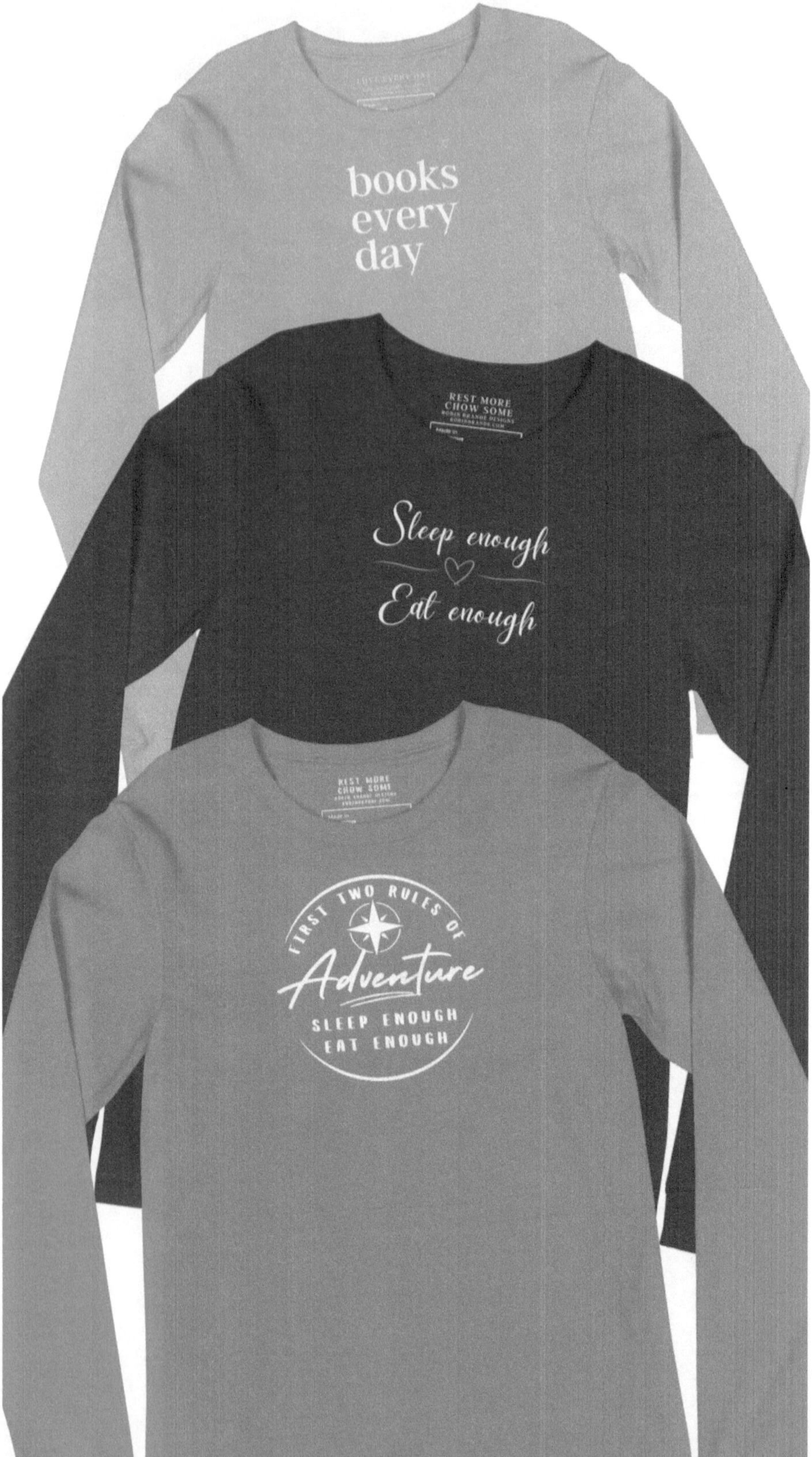

Retired psychology professor Dr. Winifred Parsons spent decades studying the human psyche as a scientist and academic. But she also explored it from another angle: Winnie Parsons is clairvoyant.

Now Winnie uses her psi talent to help clients resolve mysteries that are outside the reach of standard investigations.

The path to justice might be twisted, but Winnie always finds a way.

Life after death, miracle healings, communication with other species...

- *The Water Healers*: A nurse investigates rumors of miracle healers in Mexico.
- *A Drop of Sweat*: A clairvoyant secretly uses her skills to unravel the mystery of who destroyed a scientist's lab.
- *The Refugees*: A volunteer helps the refugees fleeing a planetary disaster.
- *The Bridge*: A grieving widow refuses to believe her husband is gone forever.
- *The Outpost Away from the World*: A scientist returns to the off-the-grid cabin of her childhood and discovers the mysterious secret to her survival.

The mountains can dish it out. But that doesn't mean you have to take it.

- *On Red Mountain*: A woman must survive alone in the mountains after her husband is struck by lightning.
- *The Rescue*: A mountain hermit and his dog race to avert a coming disaster—one that the dog senses before anyone else.
- *Home Deer*: A mountain widow takes matters into her own hands to protect the nearby woodland creatures.
- *The Gold Hunter*: An injured climber's only hope for survival is a stranger who won't give up.
- *Taken at Rustler Pass*: A teen girl fights to survive against the stranger who wants her dead.

High school senior and amateur physicist Audie Masters discovers a parallel universe—along with a parallel version of herself.

It's the adventure of a lifetime.

Now all she has to do is survive it.

Read all four books in the exciting, mind-bending PARALLELO-GRAM QUARTET. You'll never look at the universe or your own life the same way again.

www.ingramcontent.com/pod-product-compliance
Lightning Source LLC
Chambersburg PA
CBHW031439200726
48289CB00002BA/709